An Excerpt from *Khyber Run*

I threw a jock at him. "I won't wear this!"

He grinned, snagging it out of the air and tossing it back. "Then you better find some other way to keep your balls from slapping the saddle with every stride, or by sunset you'll be waddling in circles, going *meep...meep*. Won't he, Oscar?"

"Shut up, Echo."

Echo blinked at that quiet order, and yes—that was an order. Oscar had rank as well as years on this boy Echo.

I eyed the jocks. For hard riding, my father had used a long strip of cloth, wrapped to hold his scrotum high and forward. In the US, I'd worn very tight jeans for support. Now...it wasn't a salacious garment. It was a very practical garment.

I hesitantly stepped into the nearest jock. It felt okay, I guess, like it wasn't there. When I bounced on my toes, though, my balls bounced more than the rest of me. No-go. This was supposed to be for support.

The next stack of jocks felt like silk, which is unworthy of an honest man. The fourth had more give than the first. The last looked like it had been worn before, but it was certainly clean. And it fit right, cupping my balls like a hand.

"Have a spare." Oscar offered me another, black and clean but used. "Same style."

I realized the two of them were his and pocketed the spare he offered. We dressed in silence, my mind lumbering like a tired bear from the amazing fact I'd been kidnapped to the question of why I'd been kidnapped to that fine brown ass of Oscar's. And his underwear, cupping my balls like a hand.

LooseId®

ISBN 13: 978-1-61118-392-4
KHYBER RUN
Copyright © March 2012 by Amber Green
Originally released in e-book format in May 2011

Cover Art by April Martinez
Cover Layout and Design by April Martinez

All rights reserved. Except for use of brief quotations in any review or critical article, the reproduction or utilization of this work in whole or in part in any form by any electronic, mechanical or other means, now known or hereafter invented, including xerography, photo-copying and recording, or in any information storage or retrieval is forbidden without the prior written permission of Loose Id LLC, PO Box 809, San Francisco CA 94104-0809. http://www.loose-id.com

DISCLAIMER: Many of the acts described in our BDSM/fetish titles can be dangerous. Please do not try any new sexual practice, whether it be fire, rope, or whip play, without the guidance of an experienced practitioner. Neither Loose Id nor its authors will be responsible for any loss, harm, injury or death resulting from use of the information contained in any of its titles.

This book is an original publication of Loose Id. Each individual story herein was previously published in e-book format only by Loose Id and is a work of fiction. Any similarity to actual persons, events or existing locations is entirely coincidental.

Printed in the U.S.A. by
Lightning Source, Inc.
1246 Heil Quaker Blvd
La Vergne TN 37086
www.lightningsource.com

KHYBER RUN

Amber Green

Chapter One

I woke muddled, thinking the ship's engines sounded wrong. Red light glared on my eyelids. Breathing meant gagging on the seagull-shit taste of a hangover. And that sound was not my ship's engines. More like a sardine can's engines or...a plane?

Opening my eyes took effort. A plane. From the rear of the fuselage, I faced up an aisle between rows of knees hugging sea bags. Not sea bags: MOLLE-packs. Red lights in strips overhead barely illuminated a couple hundred hunched forms in desert camo, a row of males in body armor along each bulkhead, facing inward, and two rows of females jammed into back-to-back seats in the center. Male or female, each of them clutched one of those carbines the sponges called an assault rifle.

What am I doing in a plane packed with camo-assed bullet-sponges?

The plane's deck angled down sharply. Screams rang in my ears, going dull. My ears cleared, painfully, and the shrieks sharpened.

Crashing. That's what we're doing.

The deck roller-coastered up, then yawed faster than physics should allow. *Whiplash.* I saw stars. The stench of vomit wrung my empty guts.

A dive and another yaw brought more screams ringing off the bulkhead, prayer in Spanish close by, retching farther away.

How did I stay in my seat, with gravity halving and doubling and snatching me starboard to port? When the plane steadied long enough to let me look down, I saw bands of dull silver duct tape strapping my thighs to my seat, and another red-streaked silver band over my belt.

Something hung on my lower face. I had some kind of mask. No. Somebody had duct-taped a puke bag to my face. It sagged obscenely against my chin, like a giant used condom.

Pulling it off hurt. The stench blasted from it.

Where do I put this? I looked around, blinking, trying to make sense. The screamers in the middle seats were mostly army. The hundred or so men squatting in the seats lining the bulkhead were marines. Some laughed at the women. Others hunkered down, as if waiting for shrapnel to find them. A few threw curious glances at me, the only squid in sight.

A cluster of pops rapped at the bulkhead, like popcorn in my mother's big pot. One of the sponges grinned at me. "Small arms fire. Welcome to Bagram."

Bagram? A map of the giant air base flashed in my eyes, then a dim memory of riding my father's shoulder, hiding my face in his turban while a trio of *Shuravi*—Soviets—stomped an ominously silent laborer. Couldn't be...

"He means hold on," added another sponge.

I dropped the puke bag to grab my seat. The plane tilted, again nose-diving but this time braking hard. Instead of falling to the deck, the bag shot forward, splatting against a female's ear.

"I'm *hit! Aaah!*"

"God! Brains! Oh, *God!*"

"*Aaaaaaaaaaaah!*"

The plane swerved and jinked, each jerk redoubling the shrieks. The smell of fear, sharp and sour, fought with the smell of vomit.

One of the marines chuckled, despite the sweat beading on his face, and pitched his voice low enough to hear under the shrieks. "You know you're going to have to police that up, Squidward."

"No-go, sir. The doc's our volunteer."

Volunteer? WTF? I twisted to see who'd called me a volunteer, but his rifle caught my attention first. A bolt-action rifle. A sniper's weapon.

Behind the rifle, teeth flashed in a grin. He didn't seem to exist, except as a rifle, a hint of helmet, and a grin. Then the grin vanished.

The deck flipped overhead. The unsecured marines bounced, sending bellows among the screams. I hung from my seat, still taped in place.

The deck flipped again, then slammed up at us. A marine fell across my lap. I caught his weapon before it could bean him. The cool metal slapped into my hand, rousing memories like an old lover's name.

I looked at the sniper, still crouched behind his rifle, immobile and near-invisible. *Who the fuck are you?*

* * *

During a lull in the gunfire, a tall woman in a camo uniform conspicuously bare of insignia trotted the lot of us into a heavily sandbagged bunker, also red lit to preserve our night vision. Inside, a young army lieutenant and a marine corporal sorted us out and lined us up to check our orders.

I still seemed to be the only sailor. As the marines' formation took shape, I automatically went to stand next to the rifleman at the end of the first row. Not part of it, but not conspicuously alone either.

The doc's our volunteer.

The USMC doesn't have its own medical specialists, so one of us has to accompany any team heading into the field, especially for missions outside the immediate reach of an evacuation helicopter. I had, once upon a time, signed up to be a corpsman for combat missions. The closest I'd gotten to action, though, was wading into a Bangkok riot to drag out a series of stoned swabbies and one little kid who had no business being in the street at night when the bricks were glossy black with blood.

Had I been fool enough, drunk enough, to volunteer again? That might be a good way to get killed, if nothing else. Not that I considered myself suicidal.

It might also be a good way to get past the peer review, finally make chief before my time ran out. Not that I considered myself ambitious.

Some days I just didn't know what I was.

The corporal stopped in front of me, his face lit by the netbook he carried like I would a clipboard. "Hospital Corpsman First Class Momand? I just got an update on you, but all it says is TAD. What kind of temporary additional duty did you volunteer for, Doc?"

The slight sneer in his voice brought up the other meaning of TAD: Traveling Around Drunk. It stung. More so because of its obvious accuracy. "If you needed to know, corporal, the United States Marine Corps would have told you."

Rude! I could hear my grandfather's theatrical gasp. As he would have suggested, I bit down on my tongue in self-rebuke.

When I first shipped out, the week I turned eighteen, I'd gone out of my way to be polite to the bullet-sponges. They were young warriors, deserving of respect as they groped through their cultural chaos in search of something like the Pakhtun Way. But after the first six months of having to order the *kafirs* out of every fucking space I needed to work in and every fucking space I needed to pass through, I'd adopted the navy attitude. Fuck 'em. Fuck 'em all.

No, I hadn't really. It was just the hangover.

My head pounded. Worse, I could smell myself, and my stomach was full of angry snakes. And now my tongue hurt.

The corporal, who probably shaved twice a week whether he needed to or not, frowned. "Momand is one of the tribal names. So you are from around here?"

Not any more, kid. After my father was killed, then the Shuravi got my older brother and almost got me, Mom had taken the rest of us home to her family in Pensacola. I'd come back once, as a runaway teenager, only to find everyone I knew dead or missing, every place I knew changed, the language awkward on my tongue, the smells and the feel of the clothes and the very color of the sky alien.

Something showed in my face or on the screen, because the kid went on alert. "Never mind."

I didn't hear a word. That would be the polite thing to say. Instead I changed the subject. "How long has the assault been going on?"

"Thirty-eight minutes. Unless the pattern has changed, it should be over. Of course, the fact we've established a pattern means it's time for a change." He scanned his netbook, looking bored. Except his left eyelid, which twitched. "If you need to know more, I'm sure someone will be assigned to brief you."

He started to move on, but I raised my hand. "I'll need to draw equipment. Where is my gear list?"

He didn't quite sneer. "Take it up with your COC, sailor." Twitch. "Doc."

If I hadn't opened my mouth, would he have smelled the booze on me? Fine. The guy with the rifle probably had my orders. Certainly, nobody would have bothered handing them to me anytime since... My mind worked painfully and ground out a memory of being called away from a training session by Chaps, the chaplain's assistant. My face stiffened. I remembered following him out to the fantail where the wind blew hard, remembered waiting silently for him to say which of my brothers I'd lost.

Ben. The youngest. The one who hadn't grown up dreaming of gunshots and terrifying shouts in the night. Though, like the others, he had stupidly listened to my stories of *Pakhtunwali*, the Pakhtun Way, and gone off to be a scout/sniper.

Ben. The one I couldn't quite picture without a skateboard in his rucksack.

Now here I was, thirteen hundred miles, two thousand klicks, twenty degrees of longitude from where I'd stood teaching my class. Possibly AWOL. Maybe on orders. But my pockets were flat under my hands, empty.

Handing me anything—including information—since Chaps handed me Ben's name would have been as useful as flushing it down the head.

Information. I needed that first. Probably only the sponge with the bolt-action M40 rifle was capable of giving me enough. "Enough" being a graduated amount, of course. Right now my pounding head was too thick to take in much.

Gear. A knife. That went without saying. I'd sent each of my brothers a Khyber knife—handmade in Alabama—upon his graduation from high school, but I'd always used a bowie taken from my first commanding officer. Camo. In daylight, my black uniform would stand out among all these shades of dust and dusty green. From what I heard, only the paramilitary and the docs—in other words the prime targets—wear solid black. Body armor. Boots designed for rough ground instead of a flat deck. And the biggest medical pack I could lay hands on. What's a doc without his ouchie kit?

Rations. Getting halal rations shouldn't be a problem. Plenty of Bagram's civilian food vendors should be set up to take American Express. But where was my wallet?

ID. I'd need picture ID to prove my US citizenship. If I ended up captured, I needed something to persuade my captors to consider me a valuable prisoner, not a traitor to be dissected and left draped like a sacrifice over some wind-scoured rock.

And again, information. Facts. *Volunteer, my ass.* Especially for a mission here. Especially as doc for someone toting a bolt-action sniper's rifle. But I'd seen how it works; whining gets you out of nothing. All I could do was cooperate enough to maximize my chances of getting the job done and getting out of here in one piece.

The women, with their disproportionately large packs, were filing out the two end doors. The marines were standing down, unrolling sleeping mats.

"C'mon, Doc."

Being called Doc made me a target. So did the name Zarak Momand. Especially my tribal name. Nor could I ever again expect to hear my cousins' laughing salutes, *Wezgórrey! The Kid climbed it*! Onboard ship I was simply called HM1. Impersonal, the way I liked it. But the marines used a combination of rank and alpha codes on missions, so I'd be E6 Mike, right? I focused on the marine. "Don't call me that. It puts a target on my forehead."

He stepped out into the eerie starless night, lit here and there by a dim red light or by a brown smear of fire wrapped in dust. "You're Zulu. I'm Oscar. Need a hot shower? Last chance for a while."

Last chance? "Let me guess: we're heading out before I can work all the booze out of my system?"

I'd taken to drink when I realized how American I'd become. Now here I was half-drunk while surrounded by dead-sober Americans in the land of my fathers. If my tribesmen could smell me, they'd spit in disgust.

"Roger that."

Meaning we were leaving Bagram very soon. Maybe before dawn. The official line was that nothing but time removes alcohol breakdown products from the body. But I'd found that a very long, very hot shower, plus plenty of fluids, would help. "A shower sounds great, unless it would take up time better spent acquiring equipment."

"Plenty lined up."

Meaning I would take what I got and like it. "Are vegetarian rations available?"

He peeked around a corner and grinned back at me, a flash of teeth and eyes. "We don't eat the First Strike sandwiches either. Makes your shit smell NATO. We ask for the humanitarian ration packs—supposed to be halal."

Meaning I'd take what I got with the food too. And that they were interested in accommodating me to the extent it was convenient to do so. Interesting.

Still, why was I here? The navy had cured me of volunteering a while back, and I never drink when I could possibly be called to duty.

We circled behind a line of muttering, heavily packed soldiers loading into a convoy. I had no idea where they were heading, where this week's hot spot was. But unless they planned to make those poor shits sleep in the vehicles...were they heading out of Bagram in the dark?

Which brought another point to the front of my aching and overloaded brain. "Oscar, how far are we going?" *How far and in what direction and why, but let's start with how far.*

"All the way." He didn't say "of course," or "stupid question, stupid answer," but the words hung unspoken in the air.

And I could not make sense of what he did say. "All the way *where*? Did you happen to give me some crucial information when I was too stupid-drunk to retain it?"

He laughed shortly. "We'll talk later, out of this place."

"I will go nowhere until I lay hands on some ID. And a set of orders." This guy might be someone with the pull to drag me all the way here, or he might be an opportunist. If someone else had ordered me here, and Oscar just picked me up... Well, switching dates at the prom wouldn't really further my career goals. What I had left of career goals.

"Mike has your orders."

Okay, there was already a Mike on the team, which explained my Zulu designation. But I was getting tired of Oscar's high-handed tactics, not to mention the huge quantities of information he was not giving me. "You'd have had to show something to pick me up."

"You want to ruin your night vision reading that crap? Or wait just a few minutes and hear the real deal?"

When you put it that way? For right now, I followed him away from the bunker. He flowed over the ground, turning left and left again, silent as any other predator.

I couldn't match his stealth, but I set my feet lightly and breathed shallowly. And promised myself I'd do a respectable job of it tomorrow.

The plywood American construction ended abruptly; we entered a sector that felt Russian—all poured cement, heroic proportions, right angles, and echoing whispers. My ears pricked to echoes of Dari voices, Pashto voices, voices I couldn't place. None clearly Pakhtun.

I'm told my accent is Nangrahari, a mystery I'd never been able to resolve. The few Nangrahari voices I'd found on YouTube didn't sound like home to me.

I stopped, straining to hear something almost familiar enough to name. The sound strengthened, became an ululating lullaby in Turkic, and faded. When it was gone, I looked for Oscar.

He wasn't there.

Not far away, a goat bleated plaintively and a sleepy-sounding child wheedled it to be still. Farther away, a dog barked, then other dogs bounced the sound back and forth.

The wind shifted, chilled the sweat prickling on my face and neck. Had Oscar shed me on purpose, expecting me to call out like some little lost child?

I flattened against the closest wall, cold cement with deep gouges at hip height, and waited for him to circle back. My black uniform wouldn't blend with the cement wall, but denying movement to a searcher's eye was the next best thing to camouflage.

Among the shadows moved a denser shadow. My right hand curled at my belt, where the knife should have been, while I waited to identify the movement.

But he didn't speak, didn't offer so much as a silhouette of his rifle. After a moment, the shadow glided off down the sewer's edge of that too-broad, too-straight Russian road.

I followed, knowing he might be guide or kidnapper, soldier or vigilante or brigand. I'd rejected my heritage, effectively disowned my family, and was only occasionally going through the motions with my faith. Lately, I didn't give a shit about my career either. When a leaf lets go of the tree, any wind can catch it.

Chapter Two

I caught a whiff of cigarette smoke. Menthol. I gagged. Which brought up my own scent, so I had to fight down the dry heaves.

The shadow I followed spoke, so quietly I strained to hear. "Oscar plus one. Do not answer. Oscar plus one."

Ah. We were under observation. Probably from the smoker. Either they didn't know I was Zulu, or not even the code name Zulu needed to be said out loud here.

What a time to be half shit-faced.

We went in one heavy, splintery door. Oscar spent no time lingering in the doorway. I closed the door behind me without asking, leaving us in a totally dark and chill room, small enough I felt cold stone all round. But only for a second.

A keypad abruptly lit up on the opposite wall. Oscar tapped a quick sequence on it. The inner door opened to a dimly lit room with a stone and hammered-iron fire ring in the center, a young blond dropping something into the teakettle over the fire, and a flat smell of lanolin and cooking oil. My stomach clenched.

Oscar stepped in. "Why is your back to the door, Echo?"

The blond grinned over his shoulder. He was very young, with brilliant blue eyes like my brother Mohammed's. "Nice to see you too, Oscar. To answer the question I'm sure you meant to ask, there's no more fried pumpkin. There is some leftover lamb, meaning the greasy, stringy carcass of the toughest old ram for miles around, and there's onions. And naan, not too stale. And green tea, which doesn't pretend to have either flavor or caffeine. No coffee, of course, but we did pick up some more caffeine pills. Where is he?"

Oscar looked back at me. "Please come in. The door needs shutting."

I eased in, locating the room's other two doorways—both dark—before I shut the airlock door. The lock clicked a quick syncopation behind me. Sounded like two dead bolts snicking home. I put a section of wall to my back.

The darkness in the far doorway moved, revealing a man's outline. "Sorry to hear about your brother, Zulu."

Ben. The grief I'd fought off with Jim Beam hit me. I flipped it to anger. "Who are you to speak of my brother?"

Ah, that was so very rude. My ears burned. And my tongue throbbed, reminding me how recently I'd bitten it.

The blond moved the teakettle, allowing more light from the fire ring. The man in the doorway, now visible, cocked his head like he was studying me. "We're the people who requisitioned you to arrive hours ago. Your skipper said you'd tied one on, and took the trouble to explain the situation. That's why Oscar went to get you, instead of leaving you to find your way here alone—and run the risk you wouldn't."

Oscar opened a chest, took out a pair of chunky white ceramic mugs, and crouched by the fire. "Give him a little space. He ain't all here yet."

Echo poured the white mugs full. Oscar sipped one. The other he lifted in my general direction before he set it by the fire. Invitation? Or command?

I'm here enough to want answers. "What risk? When have I ever disobeyed a direct order?"

Oscar looked at the man in the inner doorway, who kept watching me. Okay, so that guy was the boss.

So what was his reason... Wait. "Zulu" meant they'd prepared to call me something other than Doc, even before I'd said anything. Nobody was assuming I'd be called Doc here. But there wasn't any other excuse for a bunch of bullet-sponges to drag me off my ship.

The world swung around, reoriented. Yes, there was.

What did ninety of every hundred *feranghi* need, more than they needed bullets or dollars? Translators.

Someone had outed me as a native speaker.

Or I'd pissed off someone who had in turn arranged to get me dumped in a war zone among people who'd been told I had a skill they needed—hoping I indeed didn't have it and that everyone would assume I was holding out on them.

The doorway shadows let pass a man with a weathered face, dark hair, and faded denim eyes. He was at least my age. "Call me Mike."

I really need to be sober for this. "Forgive my manners, but I heard mention of a shower? Please tell me he didn't mean a six-liter tease."

Mike's smile crinkled his eyes, made them look kind. "Not by a long shot. The major did us right. We can use that much in the steam room alone."

I'd been in a steam room once. Gave me a crushing headache. Didn't need to magnify the crusher I already had. "I'll settle for the shower, if it's all the same to you. You can use the time to get my paperwork laid out."

The kindness left his eyes. "There are orders cut, if you agree to them, but the paperwork stays in the major's hands. You get to talk to him, hear him out, then tell him your decision."

My nerves wound tight enough to stiffen my face. I gave him a smile I was careful to keep out of my eyes. "Shower?"

He regarded me a moment, then waved me through the doorway.

The shower had ten heads, but the two nearest the entrance had ball joints so I could aim them both at me. I stood under the hard rain a long time, letting the stinging drops beat on me, before I reached for the soap. The soap smelled strongly of evergreen and very faintly of peanut butter. Cashew butter, perhaps. It stirred memories of staring into the fire in the *hujra*, huddled under a blanket with my older brother, hand-clapping a rhythm while my uncles danced in the long winter evenings.

My older brother Hamid was long gone. Now, Ben—

The grief hit again, a knee-bending wave of it. I locked my knees and folded my arms over my chest and let it come. Like surf, drowning me. Scouring me with sand and burning salt.

Ben was not yet born the night my father got shot. Everyone blamed the invading Shuravi, but it could have been a jealous kinsman. *Myself against my brother. My brother and myself against my cousin. My brother, my cousin, and myself against all others.*

I was seven that night, old enough to join the men and sleep in the hujra instead of indoors with the women and the babies. But my mother, an American who'd taught at a Kabul girls' college until the Shuravi emptied it, had insisted that I would not be circumcised as my brother Hamid had been, in the courtyard where the men gathered.

My father had said that if he allowed her to take me to the hospital in Jalalabad for such a thing, my masculinity would be forever suspect. They'd fought bitterly, while I hid and hoped none of the cousins overheard.

The last time I saw my father alive, he was driving the goats into the mountains. Shepherding was not his job—he was an educated man who paid one of my cousins to tend our animals—but I understood his need to go. The arguing at home made us all sick and miserable.

So he'd left. So he died.

We were still swimming in grief a week after the New Year when my favorite uncle called me to leave my mother's side and help tend the livestock. Mom, exhausted with the new baby, wrapped an old *shemagh* tightly about my neck and ears and told me to stay out of trouble.

My uncle grinned roguishly, took me to the men's place, and made the cut while my grandfather and great-grandfather shot the family's most celebrated rifles over my head.

Now I was again in the land of my fathers. Perhaps this time I would find my family, would learn what had become of them. Or perhaps I would find peace without knowing.

A glimpse of movement made me fold my grief inward, leaving the plain skin envelope for anyone to see. That was the American way, wasn't it?

Oscar stepped behind me to the showerhead farthest away. He was built lean, like a Pakhtun, his glossy black hair somewhat longer than most marines kept it. His voice said Texas, or somewhere west of there. Deep wrinkles radiated from eyes that had seen plenty of sun.

My first impression made him a cowboy. A certain wolfishness in his manner, in his soundless stride, raised the next assessment: gunslinger.

I always wanted to try on a gunslinger for size. I blinked in the water and washed any trace of the thought off my face. He'd walked past my naked ass far too casually to have any interest in men.

His ass wasn't white. His hands were darker than his legs, but not by all that much. And I suspect I would have noticed if nude sunbathing had become the fashion.

"What tribe are you, Oscar?"

He looked over one shoulder, and I wondered if *tribe* had become a non-PC term. He answered anyway. "The Desert People. Tohono O'odham."

I'd never heard of them. "Like Navaho?"

"Neighbors. Here I pass for Tajik or Hazara, until I open my mouth."

I scrubbed my tongue and teeth with a clean corner of the washcloth. Ugh. At least I could de-crud my mouth. I couldn't scrub my brain, which was what needed it.

Oscar didn't look Tajik to me. Hazara are supposed to make up a good chunk of the population, but I didn't know any. From now on my guess of who might be Hazara would be based on who looked like Oscar. With his brown muscular ass and powerful thighs.

I reached down casually and gave my scrotum enough of a pinch to drop the dick.

Oscar completed his shower in the time I took to rinse off. Neither of us shaved. No razors had been laid out. I had heavy five-o'clock shadow. He had none.

When I came out to the dressing room, towel draped about my hips, Oscar followed. No modesty there—he carried the towel in one hand. He went past me, straight to a bin of clothes, hung his towel on a hook, and commenced dressing.

I turned away. Drooling over the man-candy wasn't going to get me anywhere I wanted to go.

The other bench was set like a shop's table with an array of camo in tidy stacks, all the pieces comfortably worn, each neatly labeled with a size tag. A line of new boots had been laid out on the floor before the bench. Small wads of dark cloth lay between each stack.

I picked up one of the wads. A...jockstrap? I checked two more. Jockstraps. What the fuck?

"Pick a tight one," Oscar advised.

My face heated. "I do not wear such things."

I dreamed of them. Has more exciting underwear ever been devised? But I didn't wear them.

The blond stuck his head in. "Major's here. Hurry it up."

I threw a jock at him. "I won't wear this!"

He grinned, snagging it out of the air and tossing it back. "Then you better find some other way to keep your balls from slapping the saddle with every stride, or by sunset you'll be waddling in circles, going *meep...meep*. Won't he, Oscar?"

"Shut up, Echo."

Echo blinked at that quiet order, and yes—that was an order. Oscar had rank as well as years on this boy Echo.

I eyed the jocks. For hard riding, my father had used a long strip of cloth, wrapped to hold his scrotum high and forward. In the US, I'd worn very tight jeans for support. Now...it wasn't a salacious garment. It was a very practical garment.

I hesitantly stepped into the nearest jock. It felt okay, I guess, like it wasn't there. When I bounced on my toes, though, my balls bounced more than the rest of me. No-go. This was supposed to be for support.

The next stack of jocks felt like silk, which is unworthy of an honest man. The fourth had more give than the first. The last looked like it had been worn before, but it was certainly clean. And it fit right, cupping my balls like a hand.

"Have a spare." Oscar offered me another, black and clean but used. "Same style."

I realized the two of them were his and pocketed the spare he offered. We dressed in silence, my mind lumbering like a tired bear from the amazing fact I'd been kidnapped to the question of why I'd been kidnapped to that fine brown ass of Oscar's. And his underwear, cupping my balls like a hand.

The painful place was sealed away. Mourning my brother was something I'd have to do in my own way, in my own time.

* * *

The major, a big man in a uniform completely sanitized of rank insignia, but with a pistol at his belt, ate heartily. Mike and Oscar ate with their rifles slung at their backs, no small trick for men sitting on the floor. Echo wore a shorter, blockier SAW, the squad automatic weapon. I felt distinctly unarmed among them.

Echo and the major sat on their left hands. After a look around, Echo rearranged his feet to hide his soles. He was trying to get the basics of courtesy, then. Mike and Oscar ate with just their right hands, their soles comfortably tucked out of sight. They'd been here a while.

The major took a gulp of tea. "Your records say you don't speak Pashto, Farsi, or Arabic. Why did you lie?"

Such a blunt insult had to be deliberate. So I banked the coals of anger before answering. "I was asked *once* if I spoke Pashto. I'd never heard it called that before, and I wasn't really sure, sir, what it was. Nobody asked if I spoke Pakhto or Pukhtu. After that, they asked if I spoke any Towel-head; I don't believe I am required to answer that. I do speak a little Dari, but that isn't Farsi any more than Italian is Spanish. And I only know the Arabic we use to pray."

Mike poured the major another cupful of green tea. Mike's fingertips were square, very tidy.

The major's fingertips were spatulate, like Oscar's, but much paler and with long nails. "Do you know how much extra pay you've missed out on?"

Mike renewed my cup too. I nodded politely to thank him. "Three hundred to a thousand bucks a month."

"So you paid that much attention. Yet you didn't think it was your duty to come forward. Do the words *critical need* mean nothing to you?"

I hid behind my cup, bitter and grassy tasting as it was. "Critical need for what? You want me to pray with the prisoners, or with some suspects somewhere? I can do that. My accent sucks, though. And I warn you, it's not a Muslim thing to be overcome by the power of the Word and start spouting confessions."

The major leaned forward, knotting his red-blond eyebrows. "*Why*, Momand?"

I studied my cup. Didn't he realize he'd said the answer? "I read the newspaper. I've seen the Abu Ghraib photos. I won't be part of an interrogation. I'd serve time before I'd do that."

He settled back, carefully tucking his feet to hide the soles of his boots. "Serving time is certainly an option, given the need for accurate translation. But aside from custodial interrogation, where do you stand? Would you agree to translate for soldiers in the field?"

I sipped slowly. We were getting closer to the point here. Closer to the reason I was sitting on the floor here—possibly AWOL—more than a thousand miles from my ship, wearing some other man's jockstrap under a uniform as sanitized as the major's.

But one reason might not be all the reasons. An acceptable mission might lead to wholly unacceptable ones. Interrogation, spying. If they thought I would agree to head out undercover, to spy on my own people, they had another think coming.

My own people. I'd decided more than fifteen years ago what that meant. Why now did the question arise again?

Because the times had changed, and I had.

I accepted a third cup resignedly. "If I agree to translate for soldiers in the field, y'all will document that I'm agreeing to translate, right? So then when someone can't crack a prisoner, and they decide to blame the translator and send for another, the other one might be me. So your answer, sir, is no. With all respect, no."

His pale lashes lowered. "How about for one mission? One crucial mission. You get a letter of commendation out of it. Plus a...less official attaboy."

He dangled that carrot, let me sniff it and think about it. He was all but promising me a promotion. I'd never heard of a chief petty officer being forced to translate. Of being forced to do anything he didn't want to do. Chiefs are administrators, mostly.

But I didn't know the legal or the actual limits of what they could be required to do. And the major wasn't willing to put his support in writing. So the bait wasn't worth the risk.

Before I could say no again, he added, nonchalantly, "And you'll take all that back to your nice, safe ship."

My face tightened. He thought me a coward. Or did he instead think he could push the Coward button on a Pakhtun to get a predictable response? I took another sip and forced my aching brain to consider the matter. What he thought of my character didn't matter, but what he said could matter. What was the worst possible outcome, aside from being forced to assist the interrogators?

Being sent to the brig at Miramar for a couple of years would suck. They'd probably take my pension, too.

He could dump me here, let me try to get back to my ship without assistance, let me deal with the fallout of having left it without orders being cut. That would pretty well gut my career. I'd never see chief, but the pension would be there as backup income while I transitioned to civilian life.

I looked at Oscar's carefully blank face, then at Mike's blandly courteous one, then at Echo's squinted blue eyes and tilted head. If I'd been looking at Echo when the major dropped that insult into my tea, what would I have seen in that open, boyish face?

The major looked past me toward Mike, giving me a chance to study his face. A major is high enough in rank to have ordered someone to find a translator for him. This was different. He wanted me for something specific.

And that, I discovered, intrigued me.

I took another bitter sip. "Could you list me as medic instead of translator on the reports for that one mission?"

He relaxed, his whole body shape changing, settling to a rounder form as he shed his tension. "Roger that."

I finished my tea deliberately. They drank silently with me, as if awaiting my decision. A very Pakhtun courtesy, since we all knew I'd just agreed to join their venture, whatever it was.

They'd known I would accept it, or I wouldn't be wearing a jockstrap now. "What is the nature of the mission?"

The major again looked past me. The other men stepped away from the table to the three doorways. Each turned on a boom box. One broadcast the babble of a mess hall. The others blasted a newscast and a sermon—both with voices and accents very like the major's.

The major leaned in, dropping his voice. "A deserter has taken refuge with a Momand family. Your people. We need you to pry him out of their compound before he can make his way into one of the enemy base camps over the line."

I looked into my empty mug. The major was being very circumspect. *The Base* in Arabic is *al-Quaeda*. The line would be the Durand Line, dividing Afghanistan from Pakistan.

When the Brits had drawn that line, they'd cut Pakhtun turf in half. The Pakhtun had not been consulted. Especially not the Momand families who now lived on both sides, who remembered when they could rove seasonally over the border.

In podcasts of Pekhawar demonstrations, men would often be chanting, "Are we not Afghani? Why are we separated from our brothers?" Yet the subtitles read "We support our brothers! We reject the Satanic West!" or some crap like that. Nobody in power wanted the world to know how the Pakhtun were divided or how they resented being divided.

Oscar left his boom box to refill my cup. I thanked him, "*Dera manana.*"

The major smiled faintly, and I realized I'd spoken in Pakhto.

I studied my cup. *Nanawatai* was—or used to be—an inviolable tenet of Pakhtunwali. "If your target has been extended the hospitality of a Pakhtun family, much less claimed sanctuary, the Pakhtun Way will make such a mission fruitless. You'd have to beat down every man in the hujra, including the eight-year-olds and the ninety-eight-year-olds, to drag him out. If the media find out you did that, consider the embarrassment."

Not to mention an international incident, if the Pakistani government found out.

"This man knows too much. He cannot be allowed to take that information to the enemy's leadership. On top of that, he has set my men up for punishment and shame they do not deserve. I want him brought to justice. I want you to find a way to do it."

He needed me to translate justice? "Whose justice?"

"I want him tried. I want him to shoulder the blame so my boys don't have to."

I swallowed my tea. Too much was going unsaid here. Had one of the major's "boys" talked to this man when he shouldn't have? Let him see something he shouldn't have? "Do your 'boys' deserve blame, sir?"

"My boys on duty there were insufficiently observant, insufficiently suspicious. New in country. Not one of them older than twenty. They let it happen on their watch, but they were not knowing accessories to what this man did. I'd stake my life on that fact."

"Boys." I'd enlisted at seventeen, after Mom died, to send money to my brothers while they finished high school then went on to college. Only to see them enlist, one after another, in my wake. No doubt if Ben lived, he'd be quivering with eagerness to take this mission. "I will do what I can, sir."

I wouldn't be able to do much, but I'd go through the motions.

The boom boxes cut off: *click click click.*

I looked sideways at Oscar. "I take it the hour is just about up?"

He nodded.

Taking Oscar's boom box to stack atop his own, Echo grinned. "Roger that."

Chapter Three

One summer morning, just before I turned ten, the Soviets—the Shuravi—massacred a third of our *khel's* men.

Two days later, while I was still numb with the horror of washing my brother Hamid's mutilated body for burial, my mother quietly gathered her remaining sons and our three best milk goats, donned a pleated blue burqa, and rode with us over the mountains into Pakistan.

We ranged for weeks, living on milk and stolen grain and whatever I could earn with a day's work. We rode east and south from one abandoned railway station to the next. Most of them were cement ruins, stripped of every burnable scrap of wood and every sellable scrap of metal. Some were whole but empty. The echoing chambers made me think of mosques where no one dared worship.

An old woman lived in one. She drank of our milk and told us stories of the *paryan*, the *jinni*, while gunfire cracked in the night like breaking bones.

When daylight came, we moved on. Away from the gunfire.

Wild dog packs took down our goats, one after another. The hungrier dogs also lunged, foaming and snarling, at my youngest brothers. Mom would grab up the baby and defend him with the long-bladed *yataghan*, while I threw stones and swung my walking stick to protect little Mohammed. Omar, halfway between my age and Mohammed's, usually fell in behind me, holding the little one so he wouldn't climb my back, ducking with him as I swung.

Apart from throwing rocks and yelling, we mostly left the goats to defend themselves. Once, I fought off the dogs quickly enough to retrieve most of a goat's carcass. We ate heartily for a few days. Then we starved for a few days more.

At last we found gleaming tracks and followed them to a bustling station. My mother had me sell the gaunt shadows of my father's proud horses for tickets to the eastern border.

What I remember best of that trip was the sweet, sticky rice they fed us. Omar later told me we passed through a gloriously green valley, studded with flowers like masses of jewels.

I didn't have time to stare out windows. I was busy chasing down Mohammed, bringing him back to our seats over and over, and cleaning up when he became sick. Many times, I secretly wished he was a girl, or as small as Sorrow, so Mom would do all his herding and tending. But I'd promised to be a father to him, and the tending of sons is a father's work.

At the other end of the line, at the border to India, we debarked and huddled all night on the station's veranda. The station opened at sunup, but the border did not.

We waited on through the long, hot morning. My mother squatted in the shade, brushing flies from Sorrow's face, while I kept Omar and Mohammed from bothering the madrassa pupils kneeling in the shade of the next building. I whispered the *tajweed* along with the students, teaching my brothers as was my duty, comforting myself with familiar chanted lines of scripture, prayer, and proverb.

At noon the border opened with great fanfare and high-stepping soldiers in glittering uniforms on both sides. When they finished stamping and dancing, and raising the flags, we waited a few more hours.

Finally, the Pakistani guards took a break, leaving behind only one man to bribe. At my mother's tense instructions, I gave the gatekeeper her rings in lieu of a passport or identity papers. He scraped one ring and then the next along a black stone and told me they were worthless.

He had eyes like a snake, if a snake could be considered covetous. I told him to give them back if he found them without value. He said if he gave them back, he would need to arrest us for attempting to bribe an official.

My mother raised an ululating wail that stiffened the hair on my arms. She howled for divine justice, demanding to know how she could take her sons to their father's brother now that this evil man had stolen her jewelry and traveling papers—see, the marks of the rings still on her fingers? He was a thief, a robber of widows and orphans, and doubtless an apostate!

Sorrow shrieked in her arms. Mohammed clutched fistfuls of her travel-stained burqa. Omar sucked his fingers anxiously. I stood aghast, knowing we'd never had any traveling papers. She yowled on.

As she drew her third deep breath, the mullah's students surrounded us all, shaking their hands at the border guard, chanting, "Shame, shame! Have you no mother?"

The man eyed me with respect, as if I'd engineered all this, gave me the first bow I'd ever received, and let us through.

When challenged on the Indian side, my mother shed the burqa and became an American citizen in distress. We were rushed away from the border and tucked into a tiny, white-tiled room with too many very bright lights set within wire cages.

The voice of a man echoed off the walls. He shouted in a language I could not make out. I looked at my mother, who knew so many strange things, but she shook her head.

We smelled rich fried foods, but were given not so much as a bowl of pilau to share. Omar, known as Fat Boy to the cousins, sucked his fingers annoyingly, but to his credit did not whine. Little Mohammed whined. In the next room, the shouting man switched to English.

Hearing English disoriented me as much as anything else on that trip. My older brother Hamid and I had speculated English was a secret code my parents invented, an elaborate ruse to keep the rest of the family from knowing what nonsense we were taught.

Now, I heard a stranger speaking English in this foreign place.

My mother handed me Sorrow, who whimpered unceasingly in my lap. Mohammed slanted his peculiar blue eyes sidelong at Sorrow and ceased whining. I held out my arm to him, and he leaned in under it. Omar, trying not to be a child, stared wide-eyed at me. I beckoned him close. He stood at my back, his fingertips picking at my shoulder. I didn't know what to tell them.

We had passed several shrines without asking more than a night's sanctuary. If this were a kind of hujra, where unlimited hospitality could be expected without asking, they would not have shut us in this painfully bright room.

All I knew truly was that we were among men so foreign they must be Punjabi, or even *feranghi*. Men who used English.

My mother paced, gnawing her knuckle, her eyes fixed on the door however she walked. Her taut face echoed the rising tones of the shouting man.

I gnawed my own knuckle, wondering how to get us all home when she had accomplished whatever she had set out to do. We had no horses to sell. No goats. I would have to find work, driving sheep or goats for some wealthy family, and insist on coins for payment.

Omar would have to help as well. He had not been cut, but he was old enough. Since the New Year, only my mother's stubbornness had kept him closeted with the little ones.

In the evening, men in turbans and business suits arrived, along with a woman painted like a bride and wearing the first sari I had seen. I had to avert my eyes from her uncovered skin. She took us upstairs to a cool room with blue walls adorned with photographs of elderly but beardless men, and a breezy veranda overlooking a garden.

Another woman brought us sweet rice and a curry thick with cream and yellow peas. Using barely comprehensible English, the first one told my brothers and me to eat our fill, then unroll sleeping mats from the lacquered chest over there and take a nap.

My mother nodded.

As the senior male, the decision of whether to obey the stranger's orders was mine, but a man worthy of being called Pakhtun does not contradict his mother. Especially among strangers. I bowed to she who had so gracefully guided my decision.

While settling Mohammed with his bowl, I looked back.

Our mother was being led away.

A virtuous widow, alone with strangers outside her home? I ran after them, protesting this indecency.

They stopped me at the door. They thrust something soft at me, used it to push me back into the room, and shut the door.

I looked at the thing in my hands. A plush yellow stuffed toy. A teddy bear.

* * *

Our helo took the straight route southeastward from Bagram, mostly paralleling Highway 1 and the river flowing along the northern flank of the highway.

Below us, trucks raced at top speed along the highway, leaving us behind, but Mike said the convoy wasn't going all the way to Jalalabad. Nor were we important enough to requisition a plane.

For the first hour or so, Echo busied himself with a computer, its screen shrouded so that the only light emission reflected off his face. Mike and Oscar napped. Napping sounded like a wise use of my own time, but it didn't happen.

I wanted to inventory my packs, especially the medical kit, but our sitting compartment was too cramped. I'd be in everyone's way and would interfere in their sleep. Nor could I disassemble and clean the M4 they'd issued me. It was a cut-down M16, easier to maneuver from horseback but plenty enough weapon to keep me from standing out in a crowd of soldiers. I kept looking out the window instead, even when there was nothing to see out there in the night.

After a while, a convoy on the highway below caught up with us and passed in the same direction, slit-eyed truck after slit-eyed truck, giving the feeling we were flying slowly backward.

Way ahead of us, the road suddenly lit up. A monstrous brass chrysanthemum bloomed, its petals lighting and outlining a floating truck.

The noise hit then, hard enough to shake the helicopter.

Our helo rose, lifting quickly out of the light and passing to the south of the fire.

"Poor fuckers," Echo said.

Mike's lips moved. A prayer?

What was wrong with me, that I hadn't prayed?

I stood and took the two steps of pacing the cabin allowed, partly so I could stretch—a sailor learns to stretch in spaces so tight most men cramp up thinking about them—and partly to sneak a peek at Echo's screen. He had a chess game in progress. Huh. I would have picked some zombie apocalypse shoot-'em-up for a guy like him. When I went back to my seat, Oscar moved his feet for me.

I muttered thanks. He nodded.

The helo returned to paralleling the highway, but kept moving higher and lower. Basic maneuvers to deny an easy target to anyone with a rocket launcher.

Had the truck fallen prey to a rocket or a set bomb? I peered back toward the fire, but trucks were all around it now, presenting too many lights and shadows in too many broken-up pieces to show what was going on.

A line of trucks stretched out ahead of the mess. So either the convoy had divided so some troops could effect a rescue while others hurried on, or they'd put the damaged truck on a flatbed and were dragging it to a safe place. A safer place.

Oscar returned to his nap. Mike yawned, checked his phone, and went into a flurry of texting. Echo went back to his chess game.

Cleaner light, less yellow, caught my eye. North of the river, dawn painted snow-capped mountains with orange and pink, while night still held the valley. A moment later, when dawn lit our helicopter, I took a moment facing the tail of the plane for silent prayer. No one seemed to notice.

When I looked up, I saw distant lights in the still-dark valley dividing the mountains to the north. City lights. Mehtar Lam or one of the towns on the road there. Mihtarlim, I think it was, on the last map I'd seen. I remembered how the various riverbeds came together at the narrows here. There should be a major bridge, down there in the darkness, unless it had been bombed.

When I'd come here as a teen, everyone told me I had a Nangrahari accent, so I'd come here, to Nangrahar, and from here had been pointed north. I'd walked upriver past the narrows to a series of fords. I followed a herd of nauseatingly odorous fat-tailed gray karakul sheep, figuring that whatever didn't drown them wouldn't drown me, then hitchhiked north to Mehtar Lam. Only to find the city full of Gilzai Pashtun, not my people at all.

They'd still fed me, repaired my shoes, refilled my water bottles, and put me on the back of a truck piled with sugar cane. Not my people, but still Pashtun, still Pakhtun.

The mountains had called me north and east, until I finally found an arch that looked familiar, standing beside a tower that looked smaller than the one I'd climbed on a dare. The mosque with the blue fountain was larger, newer, and the fountain had become a galvanized pipe rising from the dusty rocks, with a faucet at the end of it and a dented bucket chained to it.

My people were not there.

The elders regretfully advised me that the hajji had packed up his khel and left, under Soviet pressure, only days before the Shuravi themselves had left. The elders had known my people for generations, could describe them right down to the nearly blind schoolmaster with his feranghi wife. But no one knew where my people had gone.

New people had come, had made a home in my home.

The helo overflew Jalalabad, this country's Dallas. I couldn't see into the depths of the narrow streets, but I could pick out dark spots and guessed they were the vegetable gardens that fed the city. For every parking lot in Dallas, there's a garden in Jalalabad.

Virtually all of the city is south of the highway, on the side the river isn't on. Between the highway and the river, daylight showed fields and enclosed pasture already green, studded with walled enclosures or clusters of them. Much of the land between the tangled strands of riverbed was also divided into rectangular fields, as was all the green land on the other north of the river, to a clear line where the lush green valley met the rocky, near-barren slope of the mountains.

I felt the need to study the valley, but kept looking north into the khaki-flanked, snow-capped Hindu Kush. My great-grandfather called it the kill zone for soft Punjabis captured in the rich lands to the east. Before finding enlightenment, he'd raided both sides of the Kabul River and both sides of the Khyber Pass. He and his raiders were once caught near here, where the two rivers merged. Rather than be caught like ducks in the river mud, they'd charged into their enemy's face, had thrown a British regiment into full disarray.

He'd stopped raiding during the Second World War, he said, when a voice in the moonlight had sent him to Mecca. He'd given away his fine horses in the sacred shadows there and walked back into the mountains. On his way back, he'd stolen Shinwari horses and a Shinwari wife, and had founded our khel ten days north of her father's walls.

I tapped Echo's shoulder. "Can you get on the net here? If you get time and don't mind, could you look for where the boundaries of Shinwari land were in 1945, 1946?"

He frowned and checked. "No bars here. Probably plenty in town, though. Remind me to check then."

"Thank you. And could you also find a village or town named Yaka Ghund or Mian Mandi?" I remembered an aunt coming from Yaka Ghund, and my grandfather had once taken part in a *loya Jirga*, a high assembly, at Mian Mandi. I had a feeling those places were in Pakistan, but maybe not.

If I ended up with any free time here, some computer-assisted triangulation should help me find my old home without three months of wandering around to do it.

Bismillah, maybe this time I could find where my khel had gone.

Echo looked at Mike, then back to his game. "No prob, dude."

Had he looked to Mike for permission, or what? I looked back over the river. The water kept changing its course there, so at any point there might be three or seven or ten intertwined rivers. The little bridges looked like they'd been put together with twigs and wishful thinking.

The view from above highlighted the scars where clusters of homes used to be. For every walled family compound, at least one scar showed where some flood had brought down the roofs and walls of another, had churned the family's dreams to mud.

Could be earthquake damage. Or bombing. From the air, after a few years of weathering, the results would look the same.

People kept building there, wrecking their backs and knees farming that rich valley mud, knowing that the river would sooner or later wash them away. Looking at the khaki dust looming at the edge of the green valley explained why. As long as there was any living to be made in the river valleys, the living to be made was better than anything else available.

Chapter Four

Past the city, we flew over more scattered homesteads and fields just sprouting lines of green. The airport was a scabby-looking strip along the side of the highway. We landed long enough to let the four of us out, and the helicopter took off again.

Inside the airport compound, every building was a mound of sandbags with openings more like rifle slits than windows. I wondered if the rooms would feel as cool as caves in the summer, with all that earth packed around them.

Mike made a phone call as we walked through a sandbag maze to a chain-link fence with green metal strips woven through it and razor wire along the top.

Wind whistled through the steel wire, the sound itself chilling. The temp was in the high forties or low fifties, chilly enough to keep me shivering. Jalalabad was supposed to be tropical, more like Miami than Pensacola. And, technically, it was pretty close to spring.

The other guys weren't shivering. I resented that, guessing they had a layer of polypro between their skivvies and their camo tops. But if they had that to keep them warm now, they'd probably be sweating in the afternoon when I'd be perfectly comfortable.

Just outside the gate, a battered Chevy Suburban hauling a four-horse trailer stopped. The driver stuck a grizzled head out the window. "Oy, Mickey!"

"Hey, Golf! How they hanging?" Mike shook hands before walking around to the shotgun seat. Which, here, might very well be the shotgun seat in more than name. Echo opened the back and threw Oscar's pack in, then his own. I stowed my own between them. I hadn't yet inventoried my medical kit. Nobody was going to manhandle my pack and smash half my goodies before I could make sure each item was packed properly.

Echo got in behind Mike. Oscar waved me to the middle of the backseat, the safe spot. The claustrophobic spot. I shook my head. "I'll take window seat."

Mike said something, and the driver lowered his window. His voice was very quiet, very British. "He says get in, Zulu."

I didn't like being ordered around like a teenager. Especially not knowing the ranks around me. But they might have some reason that didn't bear discussion in this sandbagged corner of the world. I got in.

Golf studied me through the rearview mirror and pulled a three-point turnaround. I didn't know you could do that with a Suburban and a trailer, much less do it with eyes glued to the rearview mirror. He straightened out on the highway pointed west, toward the city, and threw a glance at Mike. "Would you believe they're building a golf course just north of my place?"

Mike snorted. "They've been building a golf course north of your place for the past eight years. Between incoming mortars and *buzkashi* games and mysteriously vanishing bulldozers, of course. How are the horses?"

"Glenda shows no improvement. I'm afraid her riding days are over."

"Pity. But she's more than earned a retirement."

"You need to consider putting her down. Nine horses have been wounded by small arms fire in the last few months, and others are being poisoned or fed bits of concertina wire. They're targeting OGA stock, but no one's immune."

OGA. The injured sponges I'd dealt with had few pleasant things to say about the Other Government Army, which from what I heard was mostly CIA and the British equivalent.

Mike looked out the window. "You still booked most of the day?"

The driver sighed. "Roger that. Won't be able to move out until midafternoon. If the road hasn't been mined again, we'll still get you and the beasts well out of the area before dark."

"But if we push the edge, will you be able to get home again safely?"

"Mickey...I live here."

Echo grinned. "Are you saying we have most of a day to kill in town?"

I blinked. The youth culture, the notion that the very young should freely inject themselves into a discussion between their elders, was something I'd never fully absorbed. How could people know they were overstepping their bounds when the boundaries were never made clear? I'd gone into the military partly for the comfort of having a known hierarchy, unambiguous rules that could be learned by no more effort than reading a list of them.

Were the sponges that much more impertinent than swabbies? Maybe Echo was just a law unto himself. If he'd had a college education, he'd probably be OGA.

Mike smiled like an indulgent father. "Think you-all can find something to do?"

Roger that. I wanted my feet on the ground. Wanted to see what it felt like now.

"I'll save you most of the hike, get you through the first checkpoint. Then I shall have to abandon you babes in the wood."

Mike yawned. "We appreciate it, as always."

We got stuck in a slow line behind that first security checkpoint. An SUV two pickup trucks ahead of us was searched, and the occupants' papers scrutinized at length by Afghan National Army troops.

Golf turned off the Suburban's engine and sighed. A herd of sheep and a donkey wagon of greens plodded past us. Then a bicycle-pulled wagon was waved into line behind us. Unless the ANA had a tech fetish, it seemed pretty random.

At length, the SUV was released, then the pickup behind it, leaving only one Toyota pickup, this one with a plywood gun mount behind the cab, ahead of us in line.

Golf turned the key and moved us forward. The ANA waved the occupants out of the cab of the pickup with the gun mount, though. Golf killed his ignition again. "There's tea in the thermos. Help yourselves, do."

The men lost patience, went to waving their arms and raising their voices.

"Assholes." Echo pulled out his computer again. "They've just added an hour to the wait."

Not an hour, but it was more than half an hour. We emptied the thermos, which had oversweetened black tea in it, and munched our way through a box of oranges from behind the seat.

The Toyota was unloaded and searched. Two Coalition MPs on motorcycles showed up and scrutinized the men's papers, made a phone call, removed the Toyota's bumpers and crawled about in the road checking the wheel wells, and made at least one more phone call.

A trio of young boys lugging huge baskets piled with dried sheep dung trudged by unquestioned. They leaned forward, using forehead straps to manage weight their narrow shoulders and sticklike arms couldn't have borne. I knew what their cervical X-rays would someday look like. But when the question is whether to suffer starvation now or crippling arthritis later, there is no good answer.

When we finally got to the checkpoint, an ANA sergeant with a bushy beard grinned in through the driver's window. "RSM Griffitzi! Who are your friends?"

Golf pulled a comically astonished face. "These, Habibullah? Do you not recognize the famous *chapandaz* from Texas, USA?"

A wrinkle deepened at one corner of Oscar's mouth. He understood at least some Pashtun, then, and the idea of being called a famous buzkashi player amused him.

The sergeant laughed heartily and slapped the roof. "Stay out of trouble, sir. Next!"

Golf dropped us at the edge of a bazaar. "Leave your packs. I'll put them in the tack room."

I hesitated. "I still haven't inventoried my gear."

Mike wrapped a shemagh under his chin. "What's there now will be there in the afternoon."

Echo was leaning way back into the back, pulling items out of his pockets and stowing them in his pack. "Relax, Zulu. You don't want to carry everything all day, do you?"

Then he slung the SAW over his shoulder. Next to him, Oscar slung his own rifle and pocketed ammo for the SAW.

I wasn't going to get my way. Patience, the poet said. My father's favorite advice. But I wasn't feeling real patient.

Jalalabad in the day was going to be a lot warmer than Kabul at night, but right now that wind on my ears and neck was cold. "Do I have a shemagh in the pack?"

Echo grinned, wrapping his own with a flourish. "Let's buy one."

I slapped my flat pockets. "Somebody didn't bring my wallet."

Mike looked at me. "Shut the door and let the man go, Zulu."

Patience. I grabbed my little M4 and slung it over my back with what grace I could muster.

"One more thing," Mike said. "You speak English only."

"And if I am asked for ID?"

He handed me a wallet-sized envelope. "It would be best if you don't go off on your own."

I checked the envelope. It had a typed note saying I was a corpsman with authority to carry restricted medication and giving a phone number to call, should I need to be identified. Great. For all I knew, this is what the mercenaries or the OGA carried.

The bazaar we found was disconcertingly familiar, down to the piles of rubble from the last earthquake. Or an earthquake half a century ago. Or an artillery barrage—which again could have been last summer or sixty years ago.

We found a stall displaying dozens of shemaghs within minutes, but they were of wool so coarse it might be karakul. I didn't want that against my skin.

Karakuls are born with the crimped black wool prized as "Persian lamb," but they are the nastiest of sheep. A karakul has a tail as wide as a beaver's, packed with fat they can live on like a camel lives off its hump. Dung collects in the tail wool, and maggots collect in the dung. I'm not sure I could eat mutton if the only sheep I'd ever seen were karakul.

The grit-laden wind carried the thick, sweet scent of diesel, the comforting smoke of the soft fires I grew up with, baking naan, hints of astringent herbs and fresh spices, the oily lanolin of fresh fleeces. Noise echoed, ricocheting off every wall: livestock bleating and braying, bicycle bells, horns and revving engines from the omnipresent Toyota pickups and Toyota SUVs, and everywhere the haggling voices.

People flashed rupees, euros, dollars. If anyone was using the official currency of Afghanistan, I didn't see it.

Turbans, what my family called *lungee*, were plainly not the height of fashion here. Men and boys wore embroidered caps instead.

I remembered patients, guys I'd tried to rehab for quick return to their units, calling a turban the mark of a terrorist. But where in the US getting hassled for wearing something would give it gangsta cachet, the people here would be distressed to provoke continual displays of rudeness. So they wore caps instead.

I looked for a familiar wrap anyway. If I could find someone wearing his turban wrapped the way we wrapped it, or in any familiar way, I might be looking at someone who might know where my kin could be found.

Around the corner the wind shifted; the stench of live goat stung my eyes and nose. We paused to get our bearings outside a stall crowded with well-fed donkeys, but even donkey farts couldn't override the pungent aroma of the goats up the street.

I saw a little girl with a huge scabby sore on her top lip—so swollen it pushed her nose aside—crouching between piles of rubble, surreptitiously reaching through a rusty wire fence to milk a goat into a dented canteen cup. She moved like a thief, so I slid my eyes right past her. The infection distorting her face was bad enough. I'd treated hundreds of cases of leishmaniasis, but it takes a course of antibiotics she wasn't likely to get. If she was also hungry enough to steal milk from a goat smelling that bad, she had all my sympathy.

Zarr, my father would have murmured. *A pity.*

I remembered a distant cousin her age, orphaned by some feud or other. As a kindness, Grandfather had bought her to raise as a bride for my youngest uncle.

She kept stealing food, hiding it in her bedding. Scoldings and beatings didn't stop her, but after a while my mother got the idea to hand her a piece of naan every night, to hold in her hands as she went to sleep. That was when she stopped stealing. She turned into quite the chipper little bird then. She used to sing as she milked goats in the evening—outside, where anyone could hear.

I wished I could remember her name.

A few goats would be a welcome present if by chance I happened to find my folks. "Out of curiosity, what's my spending limit, Mike?"

He handed me a wallet. "We chipped in to give you a couple of hundred overall. Just remember you don't speak the lingo until we're well out of here."

I tucked my "ID" into the wallet. "Why not?"

"Security. Basic precaution."

Basic bullshit. I hated being a mushroom. But at least they were trying to make me like the dark. A couple of hundred in dollars or euros would buy several goats, a few sheep, and a boy to tend them for a year. Which left, of course, the problem of finding the folks.

It didn't take long to find a lightweight shemagh that was long enough to wrap properly, thin enough to knot easily, but thick enough to keep my ears and neck warm if I went out at night. The first price asked was fifteen dollars. I used my Bangkok-honed dickering skill to wrangle the seller down to eight dollars, which was great fun with me pretending to speak only English and him pretending he didn't speak a word of English.

The eight bucks was a good enough price to lend sincerity to his parting wish that I might grow wealthy and that my sons would be enlightened. I thanked him, remembering to do it in English, tied the shemagh loosely about my neck, and offered the old familiar wish that he be safe, prosperous, and happy.

When I looked up, his face had gone still, the eyes chilling above his grin. He knew those words, despite my use of English. He judged and condemned me in that instant: Spy. Apostate. Traitor.

I smiled vacantly into his cold black eyes and pretended I didn't see death.

Maybe basic security precautions weren't bullshit after all.

Oscar appeared at my elbow. "Decent knives over there."

Oscar had good taste in knives. Four booths in a row had *chooras* and sword-length *salwar yatagans*, both of them the traditional Khyber knife with the straight back-edge. They looked hand forged and lethally primitive next to sensuously curved machete swords straight out of some Indiana Jones movie, and one shop's gaudy *kukris* for the tourists who didn't know a Pakhtun from a Sikh.

The shopkeeper with the better chooras wanted Pakistani rupees for them. Three to four lakh, he said. I knew a lakh was a thousand rupees, and that most of my remaining money was in the crimson hundred-rupee notes, but I had no idea what the conversion rate would be.

Before I could ask, Oscar showed me an iPad screen with conversion tables on it. The starting prices for what I wanted ranged from forty to forty-five bucks. Steep, but having a good knife was worth doing without other things. Besides, I could probably get the shortest-bladed one for less than thirty.

I picked up a midlength choora. "Two lakh."

"You are mad!"

I looked at the blade, shrugged, set it down, and moved to the next booth's machetes and chrome-plated kukris.

He called me back. The dickering began in earnest. When it ended, I had a choora with a seven-inch blade, along with a plaid cloth that would serve either as a sash or a secondary shemagh, for twenty-nine bucks in rupees.

In a warm section out of the wind, a thin man in a gray turban and a much-mended *kamiz* wept as he stood two boys on stones—ancient blocks Alexander the Great might have sat on to drink his tea. The younger boy wore a green Notre Dame baseball cap while the older—aged fourteen or so—wore a too-small embroidered cap. Their shoes had been mended with duct tape.

Both boys were trembling hard, despite their pullovers, and the older one curved his right hand protectively over the younger one's eyes. A crowd was forming, as if expecting high entertainment.

I moved with some trepidation to see the boys' faces. Instead of terrible disfiguration, I saw beauty. The older boy looked a little like Elijah Wood, but formed in the image of a darker, blunter God. My skin tightened. He was up for sale.

Or lease, I guess, since payment for a son's services normally comes due twice a year.

A woman in burqa murmured "Zarr," and another low voice agreed. "Zarra zarr."

As the Cat in the Hat would say, *What a shame, what a shame, what a shame!*

One stout man, with a fleece vest and a beard so red it might have been dyed with cherry Kool-Aid, waded to the front of the crowd. He rudely fingered the beautiful boy's shoulder and neck and asked how well he could dance.

The thin man pulled his beard with hooked fingers and cried out a prayer for guidance.

What, had he thought to sell such a beauty as a shepherd or a shopboy? Idiot. Even if he only asked the price of a shepherd, the kid would be naked and sprawled under Red-beard or someone like him in the half hour it would take to get him stripped, scoured, and oiled.

I shoved my new wallet with the rest of the rupees at Oscar. "Buy me a donkey, a good one, now. Right fucking now. Demand a full load of whatever grain the man has, too. If it costs more than I've got, I'll owe you. Go!"

He looked down at me, his shades mirroring my face. "Chill, Zu. You want packed ass, you get packed ass."

It's not funny! "Do it. Now!"

I elbowed my way to the front of the crowd and asked the thin man in English what he thought of this fine, brilliantly sunny day. Though I spoke English, my voice automatically took on the ingrained courtesy of a culture where every man is, or might be, armed to the teeth.

Which, actually, I now was.

Red-beard eyed me sideways and faded back into the rapidly scattering crowd, leaving the thin man to explain to me the extraordinary depths of his regret that he spoke not a word of my language. His voice was scratchy, tired, defeated. Yet still it held the pride and the courtesy I had so missed in softer lands.

I studied his turban as he spoke, but the folds and turns of cloth weren't the way I'd been taught to build a lungee. His accent didn't match mine either. Not the soft southern Pashto, but the in-between sound of the far north. He wasn't my kin. He was my people, though, and so were his sons. I couldn't save every kid in this land, but if Oscar got back quickly enough I could buy an extra year for two of them.

Bismillah, that grace period might bring their family back from the brink of the cliff they so obviously faced.

The boys stirred uneasily, and the crowd reassembled with studied nonchalance just inside eavesdropping distance. I'd been silent too long, and they were staring at me.

I moved closer to their father, but not close enough to challenge him. Personal space was different here; men can get closer than can Americans, but only when the niceties are observed. After my disastrous visit before, I didn't trust my command of the niceties.

I murmured quietly, in English, that I was shopping for a partridge in a pear tree and hoped he could help me.

He shrugged elaborately and begged my forgiveness for his ignorance.

A boy in bright pink plastic shoes shuffled toward me and offered, in Bronx-accented English, to take me on a tour of the bazaar.

I shook my head and smiled at him. The crowd drew closer behind him.

But here came Oscar. Peculiarly enough, he knew better than to lead the donkey. He walked beside it instead, giving it a quick jab in the kidney when it lagged.

He handed me the donkey's halter strap, and I passed it to the thin man, dropping my voice to an intimate level. "Call your son Ismail, for he has been sacrificed and yet returned to you, *fi Sabillallah*."

For a moment he didn't understand. Then he did, and his joy tore at me. He shrieked blessings on me, on my fathers and sons for a hundred generations.

My face burned. I turned away.

Echo blocked my path. "What was that about, Zu? You can't feed all the beggars, you know. There's always more."

He wasn't begging. I felt a tiny tug at my belt and grabbed a little boy's hand before he'd fully unsheathed my choora. I straightened my arm over my head, dangling him for anyone to see.

He was maybe five, too young to be out alone, and had horrible scabbing on his face. Leishmaniasis. From sand flies, accidentally imported in the last few years from Iraq.

The little thief should have fought and screamed, but he just hung there by one arm, his eyes closed, waiting in misery. Which meant he'd already gone through more horror than I could stand to visit upon him.

I set him down. "That's one family less."

ECHO WANTED TO find a true Kashmir ring scarf for his girlfriend. Mike said this was the bazaar for it. I took the sudden notion that if I did find my family, I didn't want to come to them empty-handed. I needed to bring something, and by now it needed to be extremely cheap and extremely portable. "Mike, I want to buy garden seeds."

He turned his covered face toward me and nodded. "They don't take up a lot of room. Have at it. Keep close watch on his ass, Oscar."

"Roger that," Oscar promised.

My grandmother had grown flowers and herbs in glazed pots all around the house. She'd particularly loved blue flowers. Echoes of heaven, she called them. Even if she'd died in my absence, some of the aunts and cousins would appreciate a present of flower seed. Maybe some herbs and vegetables, too.

I scanned up and down the block, looking for stalls without the overflow of cheap electronics.

About a block ahead, a little girl in brightly embroidered skirts and orange plastic shoes played furtively in one doorway. She hid her toy in her vest when men passed the doorway, but glancing back, I caught a glimpse of a straw doll and solemn, frightened eyes. She ducked inside.

I'd heard of hard-nosed students beating little girls for playing with dolls. How could a man do that?

To save her soul, maybe. When a people feels itself sliding into death and hell, it will reach for the strongest available lifeline. Around here, the mullahs and their students had been the only lifeline for a while. They were still the only ones who seemed untainted by foreign condescension, foreign maneuvering, foreign values.

I'd seen American kids her age on TV, their faces glowing with fervor a *talib* would aspire to, in the God-hates-you demonstrations at military burials. They claimed a moral purity that would be very at home here. Was it worse to beat a child's back or to twist her soul?

I finally did find a shopboy who called out to us in good English and rattled off a list of exotic spices we must surely wish to buy.

The shopkeeper, haggard and with the collapsed mouth of the nearly toothless, might have been forty or seventy. He came out into the late-winter sunlight and waved his arms—the stumps of his arms—so that his sleeves flapped like flags.

I dropped my shades and pushed aside my shemagh to bare my face as a show of respect. Looking straight at him, I wished him a good afternoon and declared my hope his family would prosper in the coming spring, trusting the boy to translate. He did, with remarkable accuracy.

The man's grin exhibited six teeth so widely spaced and dark I couldn't see why he kept them. He bowed deeply, wishing me blessings and my sons enlightenment—the polite greeting for an unbeliever.

I remembered to wait for translation before I touched my heart and thanked him. I expressed my desire that fortune and wisdom fill his house, and could he please advise me as to where to purchase garden seeds, flowers and vegetables alike, such as my grandmother might plant.

The boy translated perfectly. I cocked an ear at him but kept my eyes on the shopkeeper; from what I'd heard on NPR, looking away from the man I was supposedly speaking to would be rude.

Oscar remained silent behind me. Big surprise.

The boy translated suspiciously well.

Maybe not suspiciously well. He probably had learned his first English the way I'd learned my first Russian, but while my father had taken us out of Kabul quickly enough I forgot my Russian vocabulary, this boy was still surrounded by people who wanted to speak English.

So it wasn't necessarily suspicious. Then again, I'd always been told a healthy dose of suspicion is the best way for a Pakhtun to stay healthy.

The shopkeeper bowed from the neck again and again. "You speak to me like a man, and so I tell you as a man, do not go to Fat Ali, for he will sell a feranghi only that which is old or broken. Short Mohammed has a stall in a place very safe for feranghi to go, but has few seeds. Stuttering Mohammed has many, many seeds—fat and fresh and ready to burst forth with life as God wills, but his prices are very dear. Also, I am devastated to say it, but his shop is in a zone forbidden to the unbelievers."

And here I had to pretend to be an unbeliever. I flicked a glare at Oscar, but he looked back impassively.

I bowed to the shopkeeper. "Please understand, I would risk stoning to bring my grandmother that which she might otherwise never see. However, would it be possible to send a messenger to Stuttering Mohammed, whether with euros, dollars, or rupees, to see what might be so obtained? The messenger's efforts of course deserve compensation." Ah, no—the kid's translation stumbled on the flowery language. "I mean that the messenger's work of course deserves payment."

The wind picked up suddenly, gusting, and he paused to study the sky. Then he bowed, "The boy would be delighted to do this very small thing for you. Please allow him the exercise in manners, for the day has been long, and I fear his attention wanders."

I handed the boy six euros and a ten-dollar bill. "Your generosity reflects well on your ancestors, sir. Please ask the boy to go there and select many kinds of flowers and such vegetables and herbs as might please an old woman. No poppies. We would have trouble should our...uh...elders find us with poppy seeds."

Regardless, my grandmother jealously guarded the purity of her personal strain of poppies, which had blue petals and a generous yield of seeds.

The boy's eyes glittered, his pupils dilating, and the man snarled at him to guard his face. The kid flushed and bowed with his hand over his heart, dutifully translating what I'd said. Then he stood respectfully while the man repeated my instructions back to him, along with admonitions to go directly to his uncle and bring back enough that no shame would fall on the roof.

As the boy pelted off, the proprietor invited us inside for tea. I started to accept, but in midbow Oscar bumped my elbow. "What did he say?"

Without the boy, we had no translator. I bowed again to hide my face and told the man in English that I wished I knew what he was saying.

He bowed to me and motioned us inside, flapping those empty sleeves.

I threw a look at Oscar, to see if that was good enough for him. He didn't look thrilled, but he didn't stop me from going in.

The room was dim, lit by a break in the roof and the cold bluish light spilling in from the doorway. It looked like the beam from a cheap fluorescent tube, only stronger. To the right, a large brass dish had been set to catch the light and reflect it over the wares in brass dishes on a shelf to the left.

The proprietor raised his voice and told someone to put the tea on for visitors and not to piss in it this time.

I turned to study his wares in case my understanding showed in my face. All he had out in his brass dishes were meager piles of pistachios, peppercorns, cloves, something that looked like mustard seed, dried *za'atar*, and some other herbal stuff. No wonder he couldn't afford false teeth.

I followed the shopkeeper through the rear door to the room he probably lived in, and remembered to clear the doorway while my eyes adjusted. I couldn't make anything out, except blocky shapes against the closer wall, and the ghostly paleness of the proprietor's clothing.

I had no idea where Oscar stood. I suspected I was no more visible, though—being Oscar—he probably could find me by scent or instinct. Echolocation, for all I knew.

A match scratched against the wall at belt height. At the other end of the room, a little girl, no more than seven or eight, lit a lamp. She hurried to light a second on the wall to my right, but the match burned down to her fingers before it caught. She bit her lip and shook her hand, but made no sound.

The proprietor snapped at her to bring a twist of paper to light this lamp from the other.

I blinked at his harsh tone and looked away. Oscar emerged from the gloom, all copper and black and narrow, glittering eyes. I imagined Cochise coming out of the night, blade clenched between his teeth, and blinked. No blade.

The shopkeeper leaned toward him. "You are Tajik?"

Ah, so he actually could be mistaken for a Tajik. So then what was I picturing, if not a Tajik face?

Oscar shook his head. "*Na.*" Then he surprised me by adding more, in rough Pashtun. "I am from the Desert People, Tohono O'odham."

The shopkeeper nodded thoughtfully. "I have not heard of such people, but surely they are great warriors."

Oscar's teeth flashed. *"Ze na poegam." I don't understand.*

I wasn't sure whether to believe him.

The little girl lit the second lamp as instructed, then brought a bright cloth to spread over the worn-out rug. We men arranged ourselves on it, Oscar choosing a spot where his back almost touched a wall and he could see the door.

She brought a tray of tea fixings, then set a blue-glazed ceramic bowl between my knees, and last brought a pitcher of water. She stood in front of me, expectantly. I put a hand out, wondering if she would hand me the pitcher. She toed the bowl squarely under my hand and carefully poured a thin stream of water over my fingers and palm.

I quickly brought the other hand into play, scrubbing my hands against each other in the thin stream of water. I'm not stupid—just not used to this. Since I supposedly couldn't converse without a translator, I took my time with the washing. I wasn't sure how long it would take for the tea water to come up to temperature, but the time had to be taken up some way.

Oscar followed my cue.

The girl took away the basin, then came back for the pitcher. After another moment she reappeared in the inner doorway, stepping carefully, her wide dark gaze fixed on the teapot she held in mittened hands. She crouched and set it down in the center of the tray.

"How graceful, Noori," the proprietor murmured. "You haven't spilled a single drop. Your grandmother will be pleased to hear of this."

She glowed. Curling like a kitten under his arm-stump, she leaned against him and stared curiously at us.

No wife, however young or doted upon, would stare so openly at unrelated males. She had to be his daughter or niece then, or his grandchild. I liked him better.

Whatever the conventional rules for serving tea might be, the primary rule of a guest in any culture is to adapt to the situation and don't embarrass the host. So I took up the pitcher and poured a good taste into each of the three cups Noori had brought.

"Coalition troops inside the shop! Exit and identify yourselves!"

The little girl cringed at the bellow.

Oscar touched his heart to the shopkeeper and murmured a pardon-me equivalent in Dari, correcting himself by adding the Pashtun *Abhaka*.

The shopkeeper bowed back, then he and I bowed to one another.

By now a large MP filled the doorway of the shop. "Show yourselves!"

Oscar and I rose, hands out. He tossed his ID at the MP's feet. I tossed my wallet with the substitute ID card face up and tried to look harmless.

The MP dropped his sunglasses to hang about his neck and picked up our ID and at the same time thumbed a phone-sized device just forward of his pistol holster. A woman's voice with the soft slur of the south came from the device. "Please excuse me for intruding in your home. Alas, it is my duty. Please put your hands where they can be seen."

The shopkeeper blinked and grinned, then quickly hid the grin. He rose gracefully and shouldered aside a curtain.

Oscar shoved me half across the front room, toward the door. I couldn't comprehend his rudeness and managed one look back over his shoulder. The shopkeeper was folding back down to his timeless squat on the floor, a small chest held between his arm-stumps. He toed the latch.

Oscar tackled me, knocking me through the street door. I landed on the MP.

"What *the fuck*, Oscar!"

He didn't answer, but after a second he relaxed over me and untangled his legs from mine.

The MP rolled from under me and up to his feet in a single motion. "I guess that wasn't a bomb, or it'd have gone off by now."

A bomb. Yes, that chest could have been one. If it was, and Oscar hadn't thrown me out, I'd have been strawberry jam by now. My ears burned.

The shopkeeper cackled. "Come in, come in! You must have some tea!"

I stood and brushed myself off. "Since it wasn't a bomb, we need to go back in and be real friendly, to make up for our behavior."

The MP mumbled something under his breath. It sounded suspiciously like *Play nice*. His sunglasses were dusty and lopsided.

He'd probably landed on them. Or maybe I had when I'd landed on him. Hopefully, they weren't expensive.

He led the way back in, but immediately blocked the door by backing right out, slowly, his hand on the butt of his pistol.

I stood aside and let him by. The whites of his eyes showed all around.

"Now what?" I couldn't see around him, and Oscar blocked me when I tried to move around him.

"Now what?" The MP's voice rose an octave or more. "Now? I will *never* understand these rag-heads! I try to be respectful. I try to be friendly. I *am* respectful.

I *am* friendly! And they throw this creepy shit at me! Where did that come from, huh? Where?"

Where did *what* come from?

I squinted to hurry my adjustment to the dimness and the shadows inside the chest. My first thought was gloves. Then I saw hands, a pair of mummified hands.

I met the proprietor's crinkled, sparkling eyes and worked to keep my face deadpan. "Is it possible, Sergeant, that your recording said anything like, 'Show me your hands'?"

He swore, then checked a readout. In a calmer tone, he said, "It isn't supposed to. It's supposed to be just 'please excuse us for barging in here.'"

Oscar squatted comfortably beside the proprietor, closed the chest, and lifted it back to its nook. Dust swirled in the lamplight. "You asked to see his hands. We learned that line first week in-country."

"No shit."

"No shit," I agreed, letting my disgust show. "Now you have to bow to the 'rag-head' and sit down for a cup of his tea—if he invites you again."

"But Doc, he keeps dead pieces of his body in a box in his house!"

"*But Sergeant*, you wear dead pieces of a cow on your feet. He prolly just wants to be sure all his parts are buried in the same grave. You know, so he can be whole on Resurrection Day."

He frowned. "Islam has Resurrection Day?"

Of course: *Qimaya*. But I wasn't supposed to know too much, was I? I shrugged. "Come in and play nice."

He stiffened his back, bowed in the doorway, and asked in polite Dari if he could come in.

Where did all these people get off thinking Dari was the language this far north and east? Or had they all been trained down south?

The shopkeeper welcomed him effusively, of course, and us even more so, and called for the little girl to come back and pour the tea.

I eyed the MP. His body armor smelled dank and undersanitized. If he were a sailor, I'd outrank him. We were a long way from any ocean here, but it wouldn't hurt to take some control of the situation. "What's the problem as you see it, Sergeant?"

"Someone saw you two come in and suggested I bust up your drug deal."

"I don't smoke," I said loftily. "It's against my religion."

"You, Gunny?"

Oscar shook his head.

I blinked. Oscar was a gunnery sergeant? He did outrank me, then. He'd made the leap to chief that I hadn't managed.

Terrific. Absofuckinglutely terrific.

"So what you two doing in here? No show, no food, no booze, no smoke. The only girls in this block are jailbait."

Oscar looked over the rim of his teacup. "We don't do kids."

"And...so? Spit it out, so I don't have to write the long-form report on you."

Oscar held his gaze.

I sighed. This was *so* not the time for a testosterone duel. "I went through the bazaar and then some of these shops looking for seeds for my grandmother's garden. This shop has nothing of the sort, but the proprietor is friendly, and his shopboy speaks enough English to run around finding what I want instead of giving me the *inshallah, bukhra* brush-off."

"'Fraid I'll have to look over whatever he brings you, Doc. Best for all of us if I sort of spill out anything that looks like wild mountain herb."

"Fine with me." What wasn't fine was that I'd just invited him to sit in another man's home, drinking another man's tea. Which might be more than the shopkeeper could afford. "The dude's got to serve us tea, though, and it doesn't look like he lives too high on the hog. So find something to buy, if you can."

He glanced around, and his face lit up. "Oh, look! That stuff that isn't thyme! My cook was asking for some of this." He bought a handful of za'atar, which was carefully wrapped in a newspaper packet, then followed the shopkeeper into the back.

Sitting around the fire with the tea was going to be awkward. I doubted the MP had much training in small talk, Oscar seemed to have taken lessons in being taciturn, and I wasn't supposed to know any reasonable amount of the lingo. *So what's next?*

Oscar held his hands around his teacup and recited softly, in Pashto, a poem about a falcon.

I looked at the mystified MP, and the dawning delight in the shopkeeper's face, and remembered to look puzzled. I wasn't supposed to have a clue what he was saying. The recitation wasn't all that long, and his enunciation sucked, but it was definitely a poem, probably a famous one.

My father was a scholar. I should know things like this. I'd heard of the Prophet and his cronies passing time by reciting long poems, so why didn't I know any? My ears burned again. I sipped my tea in silence. When it was over, I congratulated Oscar stiffly, without the open admiration of the MP.

The MP shuffled through his fanny pack. "I got something y'all might like."

He hooked a speaker to his belt. A male voice crooned in Pashtun, "Close to heaven, West Virginia. Blue-mist mountains, broad and placid river..."

The MP sang along with Denver's original English, his tenor well suited to the poignant tune. Oscar joined in with a hard-edged baritone. I sipped the watery tea and worked at hiding my blush. I knew the academic argument, that nothing in the Quran forbade music—much less lifting the human voice in song—but I also knew the arguments against it. Especially for men. And my great-grandfather forbade it, which outweighed any argument.

The MP elbowed me, and I mumbled along with the English. I didn't actually sing, though. Bad enough to be associated with a stranger who had the gall to play music in a man's home.

A glance under my eyebrows shocked me. The proprietor was openly weeping, but not from mortification or helpless anger. He simply wept, unashamed of his tears. "Beautiful, beautiful."

Perhaps he meant the words, apart from the blasphemous melody? As verse only, a poem to recite in the long evenings, I tried to memorize the Pashtun version. "Shadows of the mountains, dark against the sky. I drink the taste of moonlight, and tears fall from my eyes..."

Long conditioning held my tears inside, but they scalded my eyes. The song suited the Pakhtun mood. And my mood. *I should have been home yesterday.*

When it ended, we all sat together quietly in the afterglow.

In my khel, the women played hand-drums and sang, so long as their voices didn't travel outside where a male might be enticed or distracted. Men couldn't sing, though. Nor could we listen to musical instruments. Such music was not only frivolous, but likely to entrance the unwary—as I was now entranced—and create a vulnerability the deceiver could then exploit.

Singing while listening to music was doubly *haraam*, like fornicating under the influence of alcohol, which I'd also done my share of. But the recitation says, "God wishes to lighten your burdens, for man was created weak. Do not destroy yourselves. God is merciful to you..." What could he have been talking about, if not good music and a good fuck? I just had to make sure not to die at some time when I had more dirt than light in my soul.

The girl lifted the man's cup again, and when he refused it, she pouted just the slightest bit. He winked, and she smiled. In that instant, she was the perfect image of my cousin Nerie.

In spring, we'd walked the fields before the plow, collecting the larger stones that floated up through the earth every winter, carrying them to the wall edging the field. My brother Hamid and our cousin Nerie and I usually worked together. Nerie was a year older than me, my grandfather's youngest brother's youngest child. She took my side when Hamid bullied me. When he missed some foolishness, like when Kam Ali and I threw dirt clods at one another and risked spooking the plow horse, she scolded me in his stead.

Sometimes she called me her younger brother and finger-combed twigs or bits of dead leaf from my hair. I never corrected her, content in knowing that when she and Hamid married, her words would be true.

She liked to remind me that since she and Grandmother together would someday choose my wife, I truly must be nice to her. So—to the extent Hamid allowed—she got all the sweets from our communal lunch, and I ate the most burned piece of bread.

Whatever happened to Nerie?

I probably didn't want to know. As in really, really didn't.

The shopkeeper lifted his voice, high-pitched and ululating like a prayer. His song was so Pakhtun in sentiment I needed three lines to realize the lyrics were English. "Fighting soldiers from the sky! Fearless men who jump and die! Men who mean just what they say..."

Some moments brand themselves on a man's soul. I knew I would always remember this dank, lamplit room and this thin, tepid tea, and an armless mujahid singing the "Ballad of the Green Berets."

Chapter Five

We met Mike and Echo for lunch and let our noses lead us to a cluster of restaurants.

The first place we came to smelled really good, but I took a hint from the cowering doorboy and shooed the group on past. In the doorway of the second, our uniforms got too audible a growl from the clientele crouched about the half-dozen tables inside, too bug-eyed a look from the proprietor. Echo growled back at the nearest table, but Mike pulled him out of the doorway before we had to fight.

The third place had no doorboy. Worse, it didn't smell right. I did an about-face and elbowed past Echo. The others faded out of my way.

Another truck passed: yet another crew cab Toyota pickup with yet another plywood machine-gun mount behind the cab. If you piled all the Toyota crew cab trucks we'd seen in one field and every other motor vehicle in the next field, the Toyota truck pile would be bigger. In this one, the gun had been dismounted and was cradled in the arms of a beefy man in black with a coyote-and-black shemagh scarf. CIA. Or, as they were called here, OGA. Anyone else would be wearing camo.

He'd probably paid twenty bucks for a three-dollar shemagh. Unless he'd taken it as a trophy from a corpse.

Across the street and up one building, a doorboy bowed eagerly, entreating us to come to eat clean, fresh, delicious food. I eyed his neatly ironed clothes and smiled. He opened the door and invited us to smell.

Mutton, dal, ginger, cardamom, cashews, onions, and pistachios tantalized me…and naan. Fresh naan. My stomach growled, and mine wasn't the only one. Inside, an old man threw up his one arm and called out an enthusiastic greeting.

Mike sighed happily. "Even I know that *pick-hair* means we're welcome here."

Privately, I'd bet he knew a whole lot more than that.

"Or our money is," Echo muttered.

Certainly.

At the other end of the room, a lithe young man—or man-tall boy—with heavily lined eyes danced for a group of men. They clapped and cheered for him.

The half-dozen men crouched around the largest table drew their chooras—each with a blade half again as long as my knife—and laid them among the dishes and cups on their table. They muttered in Dari. I couldn't quite pick out what they were saying, but it didn't sound friendly, and it didn't sound local.

The men at the far table kept their weapons on their backs, but their clapping and cheering lost some of its enthusiasm.

Three Kalashnikovs, an M16, something shotgun-like that I couldn't see well, and a PSL rifle with a beautifully cut-out wooden stock joined the chooras.

The proprietor pretended to see nothing untoward and waved us to take a nice table in the back. We pretended not to understand him. If we had to fight our way out from that table, it would be ugly. We settled at the smallest table, closest to the door.

The Dari speakers raised another round of muttering, but the set of their shoulders lost some tension. I knew taking the seat by the door was a sign we considered ourselves lower in status than the other inhabitants of the room, and they knew it. For all I knew, even Echo knew it. But we were here to eat, not to establish our status.

Oscar grabbed the seat that put his back to the wall. I put my back to the door simply because that would let me get out of here in exactly three steps. Echo and Mike put their backs to the room.

Oscar casually unslung his rifle and laid it on the table, not exactly pointing at the Dari table, made two minute adjustments with a small screwdriver, then reslung it and laid a scarred KA-BAR on the table. Considering how he'd sized up the blade market, I'd have expected something put out by Strider or Randall, or a fixed-blade Hissatsu. But maybe the custom rifle and the no-nonsense blade together conveyed a message he found useful.

Echo to my left had his SAW across his lap; his blade stayed sheathed. Mike's rifle stayed on his back, though he laid a wicked chisel-tipped tanto on the table. I followed Mike's example, though my M4 was a lot handier in close quarters than his sniper rifle, and laid my choora on the table, accessible but discreet.

Or as discreet as a seven-inch blade can be.

Oscar produced a small diamond sharpener and made some methodical passes over the edge of his blade. The faint *shing! shing*! probably scraped my nerves harder than the steel scraped that diamond matrix.

Tension crackled in the room. The proprietor spoke quietly, pleadingly to the Dari table. They returned to eating, though their weapons remained on the table.

Oscar offered the sharpener to me. I took it, surprised and pleased to feel a rather coarser grit on the other side, and set to the work of producing a beautiful edge.

Gunfire rattled in the near distance. My guts clenched, but I forced myself to echo the steady *shing! shing*! that had so bothered me when Oscar did it. From under my lashes, I saw the Dari table finger their weapons, then return to eating. I didn't hear the Kalashnikov *clack*, that distinctive sound an AK-47 makes when taken off safety.

Mike leaned forward. "You know, in most parts of the world, smart people hearing gunfire would be diving for the floor, and everyone else would be rushing the door."

Echo grinned. "The front wall is more than a foot thick, the sound was from farther away than this street is wide, and if something happened to come down the street at the perfect angle to penetrate the door, Zulu would catch it before I would."

Shing! Shing! "Any of you good enough to identify that weapon by sound?"

"Those weapons," Echo corrected. "Nope."

The Dari table finished eating and gathered their weapons. I turned slightly, unable to keep my back to the door as it opened, and watched them leave. Outside, two small children had a mangy goat on a leash and were struggling to drag her down the street. A Toyota behind them blasted its horn. The goat jumped and bucked, jerking the kids one way and then the other. A Special Ops guy with a bushy beard yelled at them in Pashto, offering to shoot the goat if they didn't get it out of the way. The door closed.

Echo shook his head. "Welcome to Afghanistan, where goat-pulling is not a figure of speech."

Mike took delivery of a bowl of hot, scented water and washed his hands thoroughly. "You know, those of us who were kids in the eighties knew for a fact that we'd grow up to a Mad Max world. My brother and I probably watched *The Road Warrior* over a hundred times. Wore out two tapes, I know. Back home, that reality faded. The next decade's kids knew for a fact their apocalypse would involve hordes of faceless zombies. Or worse, zombies with known faces."

He passed the bowl to Echo, then tore open a foil packet and recleaned his hands with an antiseptic wipe. "Here, we who have access to electronics and first-world medical care are like tourists in the eighties-style apocalypse vision. Like gamers in a fully immersive game. Maybe that's why so many of these guys act like children. Picture it. Within a few miles of where we sit, there's probably two thousand soldiers or semisoldiers like the OGA and psyops. Yet probably not two hundred of them could pass uniform inspection. Those Special Ops guys, now. You got to wonder how many times a loyal Talib has been shot because someone thought he was a Bearded American."

Echo passed the bowl to Oscar, then pulled out his own foil packet and antiseptic wipe. "Or how many of the Special Ops have been shot for Taliban?"

Oscar passed me the bowl. I washed, then cleaned my hands with a wipe as they had. I'd heard of cooks introducing interesting strains of *E. coli* to the wash water, low-tech bacteriological warfare, but given the fact we were going to be eating food prepared by the same folks who'd had an opportunity to contaminate this, poisoned wash water didn't seem worth worrying about. On the other hand, I'd seen some of the things these guys had touched in the bazaar, and frankly I didn't want to eat with hands that had washed behind theirs.

Oscar took back his sharpener with a polite nod.

Echo rearranged his shemagh as a bib. "Reckon the Zombie Hunters in the 122nd know they're geographically in the wrong century's apocalypse? That they bought into the wrong live-action game?"

Mike snorted. "Have they? Groups that large carry their reality with them. Faceless, implacable hordes of hungry foes who don't stop for hunger or pain or fear? Individuals that get knocked down easily, but then there's two or ten replacements? The nerve-shredding awareness that infected people look perfectly safe until after they've gotten inside your personal defenses and killed you? Does this sound familiar yet?"

Our dish came, fragrant rice topped with a generous pile of curried mutton.

A dancer came to our table too. He wasn't as young as the one at the far table, which suited me just fine. Little boys don't do a damned thing for me. This one did.

His heavily made-up eyes met mine. He smiled in recognition, and he danced for me. I leaned back to ease my hardening cock and to watch his flowing, deliberately seductive movements. He smelled and looked and moved like a healthy man. None of that was any guarantee, of course.

It's been a long time since I insisted on a guarantee. That's what condoms are for.

My cock ached for a good, hot ass. There were plenty on shipboard, plenty of them anonymous, even. But I didn't like the idea of one of them following me afterward, learning my name, maybe talking about me. So mostly I'd lain in my rack, hand curled tight around my rod, jerking hard enough my nuts bounced, imagining a warm pair of hairy buns rubbing against me.

"He probably has six kinds of clap."

The sneer snapped me awake, tightened the skin on my face.

Mike rolled naan to make a curry burrito. "Shut up, Echo."

"Seriously, I bet he does. Four incurable, and two that don't even have names."

Mike looked through his eyebrows at Echo.

The blond scowled but subsided.

I waved the dancer away. He pouted, but went. Probably did have clap, at that. And I didn't have a condom.

Besides, it was broad daylight. If I was going to lighten my load, I'd rather do it in the dark. Or at least without three marines knowing what I was doing. Probably insisting on watching my back. Laying bets. Making comments, or storing up ideas for comments to make later.

Four soldiers, US Army, came in, nodded to us, and sat around the larger unoccupied table. Not filling it, just taking it up. The dancer swam to them and took up a new dance, this one less a sensuous delight than an open invitation to carnality.

One of the army men gulped. And gulped again. He was all but drooling. Now that one would be clean, or as clean as the army could keep him, and he sure looked willing. Better, he'd have his own supply of rubbers.

No, the idiot was waving money at the dancer. The one-armed man came over to negotiate. Oscar watched them intently. Echo rolled his own curry burrito, his eyes flicking sideways on them. I felt eyes on me, though. Not Mike's. He also pointedly ignored the negotiations behind his left shoulder.

I focused on another man at the gulper's table. Yeah, he was the one watching me, all right. He was blond, with a thin mustache that was probably a lot more of a pain to keep manicured than it was worth.

I pushed myself to my feet, my gaze locked on his. "I need to use the head."

Mike rolled another burrito. "Watch his back, Oscar."

"No-go. I know where all my own parts are. I've been doing this without supervision for a good while now."

Mike gave a look I couldn't read, but Oscar sat back down. I looked at Mustache and stepped outside. The cold hit instantly, but didn't do a thing to cool my throbbing dick.

Mustache came out behind me. Looked like he'd shoved a cucumber under his fly. "Where?"

I jerked my head at a collapsed building across the street. Earthquake damage, and unless I missed my guess, there'd be a hollow space behind it, the remnants of a room. Unstable as hell, or it would be under repair by now. Then again, I was no longer the kid-goat who felt compelled to climb every building, tree, and pile of rocks in sight. The gaps in the foot-thick walls wouldn't block the wind but should give a couple of minutes of privacy.

Fuck. A hunched figure crouched there, swathed in a soiled burqa, too wrinkled to show whether it had ever been pleated.

Mustache threw her a handful of coins. "Scram, Gramma."

I translated, giving a polite twist to his words.

A hand far too smooth to be a grandmother's gathered the coins. She limped away without a word.

Mustache opened his pants, shoved them to knee level, and turned to plant his hands on the cold rock of the broken wall, near a shard of blue tile. "You got all day, or what?"

My own mouth watered at the tight pair of buns he bared. But... "Got a rubber?"

He dug impatiently in a pocket and shoved the square packet at me. Lubed, of course. At least the lube gel would be warm, body temp. My job was to not let it get cold.

I rolled it on fast, my chest as tight as the fit. Then I grabbed his buns, spreading them so my thumbs pressed to either side of his asshole. It opened and winked at me, not quite closing. Oh, yeah, he was ready. More than ready. He pushed his feet farther apart, lifting his ass toward me.

I leaned forward, pressing my cockhead against that puckered little asshole.

"Do it." He hissed. "*Do* it."

I pulled his hips back and pushed my thighs against his. *Oh, hot! Tight*! And yeah, the word was hot. I reached around to grab his cock, made a fist for him to fuck.

He grunted, swiveling his ass. "Harder!"

I set to fucking him. I pumped his ass hard, driving my rod in and out of that hot hole, feeling my balls swing. He slammed his ass back at me and forward to drive that cock into my fist. His balls brushed my wrist.

My own balls pulled up tight against me. Seething jizz hit the boiling point and scalded into my dick, hardening it. Felt like it was filling, packing in more jizz to let it spurt free in three, two—now!

My knees unlocked. I nearly fell, but held on to Mustache with one hand on his hip and one planted on the broken wall in front of him.

He bucked me off his back without a word, but continued humping my fist. I kneaded his rod, encouraging him, a wordless apology for my obvious failure to hit his sweet nut. After a few more thrusts, he stiffened and gasped and came in heated jets over my fingers and the stone wall.

I pulled up my pants quickly and waited, guarding his back, for the few seconds it would take for him to pull himself together.

"Thanks, man," he muttered and strode off. I waited a moment to follow.

Oscar leaned against the wall in a shady spot, cleaning his nails with a pocketknife. Under the concealing sunglasses, his mouth was pressed flat. No more give showed in it than in the man behind it.

I strode past him, and he pushed off the wall to follow me. Fuck him.

Chapter Six

Half a dozen horses, half of them gray and half dun, milled in a paddock behind a chest-high mud-brick wall. Two of the grays were Arabs, one of them obviously aged and one—isolated in a cage near the earth-walled shed—heavily bandaged. The other horses came prancing up to us. The biggest, a bobtail gelding, was also gray. The big gray looked robustly healthy, but that tail was shameful.

Maybe it took both gelding and disfiguring a good horse to keep him from being stolen.

The dun mares were the tough little beasts I remembered so well: sort of like a quarter horse and sort of like a Welsh pony. Mike went to the gate while the rest of us went over the wall. The horses singled Oscar out from between me and Echo, muscling us aside to nudge him. He murmured to them with rough but obvious affection.

"You'll need the smaller saddle," Echo advised me. "Want to come help me with the tack while Oscar goes through all the greeting? Can you believe he feeds them cigars? They love it."

In the heavily secured and rather cold tack room, I was happy to see an array of McClellan saddles instead of the adjustable aluminum-framed robo-saddles some of the guys talked about.

I'd learned to ride bareback. Although my uncles made money building the ornate wooden saddles used for the big-money goat-pulling tournaments, they weren't made for someone as small as I was then. In the US, I'd ridden western.

My mother couldn't send four boys through the endless procession of riding events she'd competed in as a kid, but we were encouraged to ride. The fancy tack she had won as a barrel-riding teenager had been kept in pristine condition, and the neighbors who could afford horses were happy to trade labor for riding time.

"You like the MOLLE-gear saddlebags? Or do you want the local wool ones?"

"Wool," I said instantly. "That other stuff rustles." I picked up two saddles to carry outside.

Echo dropped a tangle of straps and bits about my neck and draped aromatic horse-wool around my shoulders, then loaded himself at least as heavily. "You belong with us, all right. We ride gray horses in winter and dun in summer, because it's camouflage." He snorted. "Same saddles, though. Like a saddle floating over rocks without a visible horse under it won't catch attention."

But a saddle is a whole lot smaller than a horse and has fewer moving parts to catch the eye. For camouflage in summer in Afghanistan, you couldn't beat a dun.

Kahar, I reminded myself abruptly. The words my father used for horse colors were perfectly acceptable here. The snooty girls in their English getup who'd taunted me for not knowing fifty different ways to say *brown horse* were thousands of miles away. And if they were here, they were no longer flaunting thousand-dollar custom saddles.

And the grays were *kabood*.

None of the horses would win any conformation show points in the US, that's for sure. Maybe they could show with mustangs, though they didn't have the weedy look and heavy heads of most mustangs I'd seen. The first question here would always be whether a horse could do the job, and second, whether he could survive.

My mare eyed me with evil intent, and I returned the look. She danced out of reach a few times, but I knew that game. I herded her into a nook probably designed to trap, until I could block her in against a boulder and let her get used to my presence for a moment. I eased the bridle over her head, the bit into her mouth. She tossed her head, mouthing at the bit, and eyed me as if wondering whether putting up with me as a rider was going to be worth the relief from boredom.

While she was chewing the idea, I ran a hand over her back, feeling for any swelling or heat. She wasn't all that far behind her last currying, and that back had more muscle than the rough coat showed. With the saddle on her back, she danced again, cocking a rear leg as if contemplating a good kick. But she didn't kick.

She didn't snake her head around to bite me, which was good. I'd have bitten her back, but biting is something I think of as a stallion thing; a mare doing it unnerves me. She had plenty of opportunity as I buckled and cinched.

She sniffed my shoulder and hair then, but her rib cage didn't expand or shrink. Ah, she was holding her breath—one of those tricky mares who knew that what her groom thought was a tight girth would become loose once she exhaled.

I waited. When she could no longer hold out, her ribs caved in. I cinched the strap tight. So far, so good.

Oscar was already in the saddle, testing his mare's responsiveness to the reins and checking for any unusual reactions. From what I recalled and what I'd seen on YouTube, these would have mouths a lot harder than I'd become used to.

She planted herself, bracing against my pull a few times. I let her. That wouldn't last. She rolled her eyes at me, ears back. But she didn't kick.

I checked the buckles and ran a finger under the edge of the saddle and the cinch, admiring the smooth lay of both, and grinned at Mike. "It fits like it was made for her."

He swung into his own saddle. "Roger that. She was bought to fit the saddle. How does it fit you?"

I shortened the stirrups, then swung up. "Like it was made for me."

Oscar scowled. "Close enough."

What? What's eating you?

He took off, raising a cloud of dust like some black hat in a movie. I held my mare in, though she danced with eagerness to follow. Echo's stocky little mare jittered beside me, but Mike wasn't up and settled yet.

No, Mike was down and checking his girth.

I wouldn't have mounted before checking my girth. But voicing that little fact would do no one any good. Mike also made a point of checking his mare's feet, then mounted again. His brows knotted. "Watch me a minute. Is this mare's gait uneven?"

I watched him for only a few steps before I called halt. "She's favoring her off rear leg."

He swung down, scowling, and ran his hands down the favored leg. "I thought so. I can't feel anything, but the old girl's probably not up to mountain scrambling. Help me catch the gray gelding with the bobbed tail, please. This saddle fits him real well too."

I wondered again about the bobtail. My grandfather and uncles gloried in their horses' long, sweeping tails.

Oscar came cantering back. "OGA with tack."

The corral had only the one unclaimed horse sound enough to catch anyone's interest.

"Shit," Mike said succinctly, flipping the halter off his mare's ears and tossing it in Oscar's direction. "Grab Bob."

Oscar backed three paces and jumped the corral wall like it was waist high instead of chest high. I urged my mare close to the wall to watch him approach the gray and snag the halter neatly over its head. He leaned over and bucked the halter and led the horse to the gate.

He looked over the wall at me. "Face covered, mouth shut. Even if they take you, I'll get you back. Count on it."

I heard the theme song from *Terminator* and turned slowly, holding in my suddenly antsy mare more with my legs than my hands. Why might they take me? And why *I'll* get you back, not *we'll* get you back?

Five men, their faces concealed by shemaghs that covered everything but their Oakley sunglasses, piled out of the crew cab of—surprise!—a Toyota pickup! The driver and the gunner standing behind the cab held their positions.

The five who came out moved like their joints were all loose, like stoned cowboys, and every one wore a pistol harness. "Y'all can dismount now, fellahs. We need these horses for the day."

"They're not for hire, sir," Mike said crisply. "They're my personal property. Some ID, gentlemen?"

The guy in the lead struck a hipshot pose. "Then we're commandeering them. Buying them, if you prefer. Either way, get down. We have a curtain call half a mile away in fifteen minutes."

Echo maneuvered between me and them, his machine gun off his back and laid casually over one thigh. His poorly tied shemagh caught the wind and whipped against his face.

Interesting. He had a free hand and a gun hand. His mare didn't need reining for guidance.

"I still haven't seen ID," Mike observed.

The loose-jointed men flipped open ID wallets. I couldn't see anything of what was in them, but the men flipped them shut again with supreme confidence. The one in the lead cocked his head. "I'm guessing you're an NCO, am I wrong? 'Cause if you are, I outrank you."

Mike gave a slight tilt to his head, and they went for their guns.

In the clatter, Mike raised one hand. "You don't want to do this, and for the record, it doesn't matter what your rank is. I don't care if you're CIA, Special Ops, or sanitation engineers. What matters these days is the rank of the top guy who's willing to put his ass on the line to back you up in whatever you're currently doing. I'm guessing your boss is not as intimately acquainted with your mission as mine is with mine. Who you wanna call?"

The guy in the front pulled down his shemagh to show his grin. Perfect white teeth. They looked fake. "You guess wrong. We have orders from on high: Put 'Nice American' face on for any local charity do-wah-wah that comes up. Especially this one, since CNN is setting up their satellite feeds now. There will be a Coalition presence. But guess what? We need horses, and we need zero risk of some rag-head fanatic with tears running down his face jabbering on CNN about how we stole his horses, just when he bizmah-fucking-lah needed them to take a load of sheep turds to the bakery. And these here are the only registered US-owned—"

"Personally owned!" Echo snapped.

Don't interrupt the elders. I chided him mentally.

"What *ev*-ah, Blondie. We have the authority to confiscate your left nut if we want it, but—lucky you!—we only want the horses. If you're white about it, we might even return them this evening."

"Dismount," another clarified. "Or face immediate arrest."

I caught a flicker of movement and turned. Oscar was handing something book-sized over the wall of the corral. He gestured past me. I took the thing—an iPad mirroring my masked face—and then the sky and handed it to Echo. He snorted softly and passed it on to Mike.

"Drop it or lose a kneecap," someone snarled.

Mike angled the screen at them. "Smile, boys. You're on live feed. Eleven hundred viewers now, and no telling how many more coming in over the next thirty seconds. Especially if things get exciting."

"Bluff," a man in the rear muttered. One of them, maybe the same one, whipped out a phone the size of a deck of cards and went into thumb-typing overdrive.

The faceman looked at Mike's screen, his smile losing its smug menace. "As I was saying, soldiers, the children's burn ward will have to close tomorrow unless our contributions can keep it open. The Coalition has organized a game of buzkashi, the national game here in Afghanistan, in order to raise enough money to keep the children under medical care, to give them some relief from the unspeakable pain and scarring. No little kid should suffer that kind of pain."

The thumb-typer showed him a screen, and he took off his sunglasses to smile again. This smile oozed insincerity, which I hope transmitted well. "We deeply appreciate your volunteering your horses to allow us to field a team. The need is critical; the need is now; and surely the children's cries would melt your heart."

"No man forks my horse," Mike drawled, "unless I trust him. If the Coalition needs my horses, they get my men to ride them. Sorry for any confusion you *gentlemen* might have suffered, but if you boys want to ride, you can bring your own mounts. Lead the way."

Echo looked past me at Oscar. I threw a glance back too. His face was invisible behind sunglasses and shemagh, and neither hand was visible. His rifle's muzzle didn't project from behind his shoulder. So Echo wasn't the only one with rifle in hand.

Echo eased his mount toward mine, surreptitiously pushing me out of the line of fire.

Were they always this paranoid, or was I missing something? Best to go with their instincts instead of the ones I'd let get dulled with too many years on ships.

The faceman tried to catch Mike's bridle, only to find Mike's arm in the way. "You can't seriously mean to play instead of us. This is a very rough game. Injuries are expected. We don't have time to train you!"

"Nor I you," Mike pointed out. "You cannot have my horses, which are personal property and specially trained. Didn't you say fifteen minutes? How far do we need to ride to get to the game? You don't want the US team to lose by default, do you?"

Chapter Seven

The field was maybe half a mile long, with rapidly filling stadium seating along one side, right in front of the circle of justice. It seemed small, but I hadn't been on a game field since I was nine, so what do I know? The camera trucks were clustered, the cameras pointing at the stands, the mountain backdrop, or the goalposts. But the real goal was here in the middle, the circle of justice where all men must come.

"We were scheduled to use the other field," the CIA faceman told Mike, "but the bomb dogs found an old land mine, probably dating to the eighties. Couldn't have been alive or it'd have gone off long ago, so we suggested running a junker of a truck over it, but some lard-brain who expects to collect his retirement someday decided the field wasn't *sa-afe*."

He hawked and spit. At least it wasn't tobacco spit. "We told him this field was proven safe. About a hundred of them were playing buzkashi here Monday, and nobody's hooves got blown off. If you're worried, of course, we can take your places."

Mike shook his head.

I kept trying my mare with knee pressure here or a weight shift there. When a rider doesn't have time to train the horse, all he can do is educate himself as to what actions cue the animal to do what. I leaned way far down my right leg. She stopped dead, as she had before, only moving when I settled in the saddle and urged her forward.

I didn't know who'd trained her, or for what, but that was one trick I was glad to learn about before I had a field full of riders pounding toward me and a calf or goat at the end of my arm.

Not that I was going to make a goal if we were playing against real chapandaz. I used to be a good rider, and I put in gym time six days a week, but I'm not delusional.

The faceman appeared beside me. "Nice stretch. Have you played before?"

Oscar's mare danced, and inserted her broad butt between my horse and the CIA man. I shrugged, not needing that unsubtle hint. Let Mike tell these people whatever Mike wanted them to know.

More than a hundred horses ranged the field in clusters. Mike parked us near a truck and rode over to where the cameras and the official-looking people were gathered. A voice over a speakerphone said CNN wanted each team limited to six players so the cameras could keep track of the action. Meaning we didn't have a team to field anyway. How was Mike going to play this?

Echo's mare danced, as did mine. He kept looking right and left, trying to take in everything at once. "The Net calls it roller derby on horseback. I can't wait."

He talked like a beardless boy. Naturally. He was a beardless boy. I wasn't. No point in letting every watcher know how much excitement bubbled along my nerves. So I tried to smooth out my movements in hopes this would calm my mare.

I'd seen some games up close, riding—as boys did—along the outer edge of the action, careful to stay out of the way. It was how a boy learned here. Since then, I'd watched games on TV and podcast, though usually whoever was narrating the action had little idea of what was going on. In a real game, with twenty-plus players and with twice that many trainees and cheerleaders on horseback racing up and down the edges of the field, I'd never get close to the *boz*.

When Mike returned, he took custody of our saddlebags and packs and bowed out of the action. His gelding was barely three years old, he explained now that we were well away from the paddock with the deceptively hearty-looking mare, and not schooled in the skills needed for this game.

Echo's voice took on a sound suspiciously close to a whine. "Whose team are we on, then?"

"The first one to play," Mike said sharply.

Echo's exposed ear reddened.

Three Canadians dressed for cold weather rode by on thick-legged shaggy geldings. Mike whistled, and they wheeled in unison. Their horses stepped toward us in unison.

"Our teammates, or rather yours. Canadians. They want to win," he added regretfully.

The tallest Canadian, in a black shemagh, brandished a fistful of red cloth. "Hello, Meeshell! Hello Osskah! Echo! Et Zul-you! I am Anjou! He is La Salle, and she is La Teton—tell no one! We hope you can keep up, eh?"

The cloth he handed me turned out to be a red vest, assembled with a stapler rather than stitches. The first good yank would remove it. Which was probably the point.

Mike's abdication and the even divide between us and them could leave a vacuum in leadership. My guess was that Anjou would step into the vacuum, unless Oscar did.

Normally the elders of the team direct the action, letting the younger players struggle over possession during the brutal race to a goalpost and back.

The elders take the boz only for the final few steps to drop it in the circle of justice. They're fully as fierce as any boy on the field, but wise enough to let the boys take the damage. Any man with a white beard has usually had at least one long and sincere discussion with his own back. And the boz is a heavy thing for an older man to lift and sling. Even if this one was a goat instead of a calf.

Mike shortened his gelding's rein. "For our team to win, the boz has to go around the north post then be brought back to the middle and dropped in the circle. For their team to win, the thing has to be taken around the south post and brought back to the circle. Nobody can trip your horse, deliberately hit your hand, or deliberately knock you off your horse. There's no rule against accidents, which is why they have those helmets and club-handled whips. Nor is there any rule against a face punch or a kidney punch.

"You Canadians have whips—good for you. You'll be the defensive players. Whoever gets hold of the goat, sling it over to Oscar here. He won't drop it. Once he has the goat, everybody cluster around him and ride hell for hot leather. Questions?"

"Have any of you played before?" The woman's voice was low, but not too low to carry a challenge.

We looked back at her. Her gelding shook its heavy head. She shoved her arms through a red vest. "*Merde.*"

The males flanking her laughed. Shemaghs and shades completely hid their faces, but their body language spoke clearly. They would be a team, and what they wanted from us was to stay out of their way.

Anjou twirled his whip, which looked locally made. "Listen. When a man grabs the goat, it is wet. The hair, it can slide right off the skin. Grasp not gently. Never gently. I have once played, so among us, I am master."

"Ooh la la, ooh rah!" Echo laughed, and his mare half reared.

The Canadians glanced at each other.

A mounted phalanx charged us. We scattered like a pack of dogs. They reassembled beyond, perfectly posed against the bare-mountain backdrop, and fired their AK-47s into the sky. "We are Afridi! You are geldings who ride mares! Play against bearded men! Or slink away and hide behind your shameful women!"

Nobody dived for cover. I looked around. Only the media were even looking in their direction, and not all of them were.

I hid my smile under my shemagh.

Mike was talking to an unveiled woman who looked a lot like Condoleeza Rice. She was dressed in slacks, instead of showing her bare legs, but her neckline was more suited to the weather and the camera's eye than to the cultural norm. He turned away. She grabbed his bridle. Looked like she was arguing with him.

Echo nudged me. "Translation?"

"The Afridi have testosterone. We have loose women." I leaned over and retied his shemagh.

"You need to do this where I can see," he complained. "I keep guessing, and the stupid thing keeps unwinding any way I tie it."

I smelled his deodorant. Axe, I thought, and wondered why Mike had let him wear a scent that would identify him as NATO to anyone downwind.

One of the Canadians snorted. "You need to be smarter than the rag, eh?"

You have to be smarter than the tie, Ricky. My mother's father had stood me in front of a mirror and reached around from behind to knot my necktie. *Half-Windsor like this if it's too short for a full Windsor.*

I felt guilty, not missing the old man. Even if he had done his best to make apostates of my brothers and me. I think he'd succeeded with my brothers. One more reason they were all better off without me. I wasn't a good Muslim, but I'd never be anything else.

Mike evidently won his argument; he cantered over and advised we had the first match, against half a dozen Tajiks in fur-trimmed helmets and riding long-legged stallions. Two of them looked my age, two looked older, with white-shot eyebrows but probably were my age, and one had bushy white eyebrows. Real chapandaz. So much for getting close to the boz.

I looked at Oscar. "We're about to get slaughtered."

He tightened his rifle strap. "So?"

He didn't care? How could a man not care about winning?

Mike's voice hardened. "I don't have to ask you to make a good show. You're marines. But remember your mission. Your primary objective at this point is to avoid injury to yourself or your mount. Your second is to avoid maiming or killing anyone else, because we don't have time for the paperwork."

Echo's horse gave another half rear. Not exactly the sign of a confident mount with a calm rider, was it? But unless he fell and broke something, it wasn't likely to be my problem.

The chapandaz looked at our mares, at the Canadians' geldings, and curled in on themselves to smother their laughter. Real chapandaz rode only stallions.

To make a better show, the camera guys insisted on backing us all about fifty meters off the circle of justice. The starter stood straddling the boz, a black goat. He raised a pistol and, amid cries of bismillah, fired a red flare.

Then he ran for his life, knees high and fists pumping.

Echo and the Canadians charged the boz in a flying wedge. I rode enveloped in their dust, with Oscar beside me. The chapandaz waited until a Canadian lifted the boz from the ground, then bowled over his horse, took the boz, and galloped for their post.

Echo rose in his stirrups, yipping like some kind of movie Indian, and raced forward. Coming abreast of the chapandaz, he lunged for the boz, and caught a lash across the face.

He yelled, then jumped to squat with his feet on his saddle, and snapped a kick at the nearest rider. The rider ducked, but the kick caught him high on the shoulder. He went down in the churning dust.

I yelled like a madman, the sound drowned in thousands of other yells and cheers. Talk about a foul—a *magnificent* foul!

The riderless horse stopped dead. Another Tajik horse danced aside to keep from trampling the downed rider. The third one leaped—or bucked, I wasn't sure. I had no clue who carried the boz.

Echo was now grappling bodily with one of the chapandaz. A Canadian charged laterally through the mess, wheeled, and came back at us with the black bulk of the boz under one leg and his whip between his teeth.

I pirouetted left, Oscar pirouetted right, and we laid down a gallop toward our goalpost. As the Canadian caught up with us, we opened to sandwich him.

Then the post was there. I thought of circling short, but if I did, someone might argue I was the one carrying the boz and that it hadn't circled the post.

Oscar wheeled about the post. The Canadian flanked him, and I rode the outer circle, urging my mare to keep up and then to plunge ahead to break up the clump of chapandaz blocking our way. My mare, not being trained as a four-legged fullback, shied to one side and dived between a pair of the big stallions.

A whip slashed across her nose.

She reared, screaming, then slammed all her weight onto her front hooves and lashed out with her rear hooves. My spine whip-cracked all the way up and down, and my teeth snapped shut.

One rein snaked out of my hand. I pulled the other to my knee, but the mare crow-hopped and bucked in a tight circle. All I could do was hold on.

I was vaguely aware of the chapandaz muscling red-vests to one side of the circle of justice and tearing off toward their own goalpost. It probably took only seconds to settle my mare, but a couple more to get the reins in hand. By then, eight horses were thundering in my direction, dust boiling about them.

Oscar and his mare stood solidly beside me. He nodded. "Come."

Roger that.

Now we had to intercept the boz. It had circled both posts, so whoever threw it into the circle of justice would win.

We charged the coming mass, and it split around us. A Canadian had the boz again, and Echo had a Tajik-style club-whip. Echo twisted to his left and slashed his whip at a chapandaz. Someone's knife went spinning high into the air, a nice image if CNN could catch it.

A Canadian with blood soaking his shemagh rode beside me, his leg jogging against mine. His horse stumbled.

I automatically pressed my mount to the left, so she wouldn't fall with his, just as he slung the boz at me. "*Allez! Allez!*"

I caught one leg, with broken bone jutting through the hide, and dragged the front end of the carcass over my pommel, leaning in the opposite direction to try to balance the weight. The hide tore, sliding the slick mass back over my thigh and down my leg. I fumbled for a better grip.

Horses and men surrounded me. Whips and fists came out of the dust.

I leaned sharply over the carcass, and my mare stopped dead. The other riders plunged on, then entangled one another as they turned to get at me again.

Oscar reached across my saddle and into the neck of the boz, found something to grip, and dragged the lumpish mass squarely over my pommel. "Go!"

We rode together for the circle, barely visible in the hoof-churned dirt, and flung the broken carcass down.

My mare huffed and blew wads of brown-stained foam. I slid down and grasped her halter, anxious to inspect the mud-crusted whip-cut across her nose. The tender skin had welted, but wasn't bleeding so much as seeping a bit.

I felt the bones gently, working from the side to make sure any pain would be from the bones, not from the bruised skin. She seemed all right.

Two oozing welts decorated the back of my left hand. I couldn't recall being struck.

Someone was at my back. I turned, but it was Oscar, his back to me, facing a mob of chapandaz, the fox-hatted Tajiks in front. Their faces were animated, amazed; they kept bowing to look under the mares. "Mares? *Mares?*"

"Tatar mares," I said, remembering to use English. "Very fast, but not so strong as yours. In a long game, you would win."

They grinned. "Very fast. Very fast."

Then they switched to their language, chattering at me and at Oscar. I felt no threat from them. They'd been shamed by a loss to nonstallions, but were far enough from home to hope no one who mattered would ever hear of it.

Another group of riders now surrounded Echo; they'd pushed back his shemagh and fingered his short gold hair, talking. He had one hand on his wallet pocket and one on his weapon, but he grinned and let them paw him. I saw his empty knife holster, but for all I knew he could have lost it when doing that kick.

A woman with a camera elbowed in through the crowd. The chapandaz sprang away as she passed. She thrust a microphone into Echo's face.

I watched the chapandaz, amused by how the woman's forwardness stunned them. Maybe they thought she was Echo's wife.

Then I remembered the bloody-faced Canadian. Some cameras had focused in on the three of them, and the bleeding one was still wearing his shemagh. For right now, I was their doc. I should be handing Oscar my reins and making my way over there, to see whether the injury required urgent attention.

But a man in a sanitized camo uniform and a shemagh like Mike's was leading Mike's overladen gray gelding daintily among the power cords and clusters of newspeople. And Oscar, who had shed his red vest, was pointing his face at me, jerking his head in a way that probably didn't mean *my neck is stiff*.

I swung up into the saddle, tossed my red vest into the crowd, and followed Oscar around the back of a CNN trailer, trusting Mike to extract Echo, and leaving the Canadians to handle any prizes or interview requests.

We rode between clusters of horses and riders, enough to fill the day with five-minute mini-matches. I heard the CIA faceman's voice. The OGA men were flashing ID at a group of riders with stunned, disbelieving faces. The riders were all officers, though, and should be able to take care of themselves.

Oscar startled me by heading down a tight alleyway, one built for ambush. His mare broke a trot.

I could follow, or I could head back into the crowd and look for Mike. Given the number of uniforms, shemaghs, and horses, the chances of finding Mike and Echo were pretty slim. So I put my heels in the mare's flanks and leaned forward.

We emerged from the alley at the edge of a bazaar.

Sullen, deeply lined faces looked up at us from the closest booths. Not a hand showed. A metallic rattle punctuated by many hard *clacks* echoed off the scarred buildings, safeties being taken off dozens of unseen weapons.

Our mares slowed to step carefully, avoiding insult and assault by what felt like a breath here and a few inches there. The wind whistled through ropes and cables and up my sleeves and down my collar, finding all the sweat from the game and chilling it.

I shivered and didn't bother to hide the fact. I was too busy watching for the slightest signal, the rise of a leader who would cry for the death of the infidel, the foreigner, the invader.

Two horsemen waited at the far edge of the bazaar: Mike and Echo. We joined up without a word and stopped half a mile later to rearrange the baggage. Then we quietly rode east to rendezvous with Golf and his trailer.

Only after we stopped in a parking lot did I notice Echo's reins tied loosely and lying on his lap. His gun hand was fine, but the other had swollen so much his fingers looked like meat balloons. The two on the pinkie edge of his hand stood out at the wrong angles.

"You did have the option of requesting medical attention at any time," I scolded.

"Yeah." He dismounted gingerly, holding the hand out. "Can you still fix it?"

Rapid swelling was a bad sign, but some of it might be attributable to his excitement level. I pulled down my medical kit. "Did you feel or hear anything snap?"

"No, sir."

Sir? He was in pain, then. He hissed as I touched each finger, feeling out the injury, but didn't jerk away. I couldn't be certain with this much swelling, but it felt like a simple dislocation of his pinkie and ring finger. A little jab of morphine would help, but I didn't know if any had been packed, did I? And every moment's delay would increase the severity of the swelling, the chance of complications.

"You're not going to yank on it, are you, Doc?"

"No. I'm going to assume you're an adult and can cooperate in your own treatment. Pull very slowly and smoothly against my pull, okay?"

I laid his hand across my thigh, took a grip, and pulled the digits straight out, stretching the tendons to maximum and using my other hand and thigh to press the butt ends of the two dislocated bones into place. One slid smoothly into place but the other gave a little snap.

"*Fuck!*" He spasmed against my shoulder.

I held pressure a moment, for pain control, then eased up. I'd never done two fingers together before, but the most cooperative patient wasn't likely to hold still twice.

Out here I couldn't send him through ultrasound to make sure everything had gone back in place, and that no bones had chipped or cracked lengthwise. But from what I'd seen, the degree of swelling he maintained tomorrow would be a reasonably accurate indicator.

If he couldn't use the hand tomorrow, I'd send him home for surgery. I may not be a physician, but I'm a doc, and I can do that.

Meanwhile, there were consequences to address, and if that medical kit didn't have some splints at the very least, it wasn't worth carrying. I moved Echo's hand to his own lap. "Don't move."

Mashallah, splints of all kinds. I selected two glorified Popsicle sticks and a roll of self-adhesive stretchy tape. Another section of the kit had ibuprofen, Decadron, and Tylenol#3 along with the forms to document each tablet of that last. "Have you ever had an adverse reaction to a painkiller or to any medication?"

"Not allergic to nothing, Doc."

Mike's shadow fell over him. "Zulu."

"Sorry. Zulu."

I kind of liked Mike for not fucking with the kid until his fingers had been fixed. And I took a perverse pleasure in signing the controlled substance sheet *Zulu*.

I made Echo eat a squirt-pouch of cheese over a retort brownie so the pills wouldn't hit an empty stomach.

Then, while Echo played with something he found extraordinarily funny on his computer, I learned my way around the rest of the medkit. It was nonstandard in all the right ways and good in every other way, except there was neither morphine nor any effective equivalent. I guess having to track and account for a narcotic would probably ratchet the paperwork to a higher level than anyone wanted to deal with.

I had also inventoried and rearranged my assault pack by the time Golf arrived with his horse trailer.

Chapter Eight

Chunks of the road had broken away every few yards. To anyone who insisted on staying in one lane, the road would be impassable, at least without doubled tires or treads.

Golf soldiered on, driving on the left here and on the right there, sometimes driving down the middle while Toyotas and bicycles and donkey carts swerved left and right around him. He recited *zaboor*—psalms—in English under his breath the whole way, so quietly only two or three words at a time reached me in the sweaty center of the backseat. Beside him, Mike held a pistol on his lap and his rifle between his knees.

Golf swerved to pass a troop of camels bearing rolls of carpet, with a heavily robed woman in purple riding atop each stack of carpet rolls. Some of the women shouted at him as he squeezed past. One urged her camel into a trot to intercept us, then flung a dish of fresh sloppy-wet dung onto the windshield. Golf hit his wipers and his horn and blasted through.

Camels don't drop turds that wet. Nor does any healthy animal I knew of. Low-tech biological warfare. From Golf's white-lipped face, he knew.

In the backseat I clenched my teeth and waited for an explosion or a bullet through the glass. Or a scream from the trailer saying a bullet had found one of the horses.

Echo bounced in his seat. "How long was she carrying that fresh shit, waiting for someone to pitch it at? You got to wonder."

"Shut up, Echo."

"We could have ridden this far by horseback in half the time, I bet. Why didn't we, huh?"

Mike half turned in his seat. "What the fuck is wrong with you?"

"I just wanna know why!"

Golf circumnavigated another crater. "Von Steuben said what makes an American soldier different is the need to tell him why. In some of the districts we've passed through, NATO horses would have been shot, if not hamstrung by some bleeding ankle-biter in the street."

Then he went back to his verses.

Late in the afternoon, we'd finally navigated all the way across the green farmland on the other side of the river. At the khaki foot of the mountains, Golf let us unload.

For a man who said he wasn't afraid to be out after dark, he was gone with a quickness.

* * *

We rode on while the sun set behind the mountains, and kept going even after the lingering sky glow faded, to find a caravansary Mike and Oscar knew of. We found it with the scent of peppers, garlic, cinnamon, and tomatoes cooking. The two eastern corners of the structure had been reduced to rubble, along with the wall between them. What was left was a shallow *U* shape with two partial walls facing one another and a whole wall connecting them.

There was a fire near the southwest corner, with five men about it, and horses were clustered in the middle of the west wall.

Mike pulled a small scope from a belt pouch and studied the men about the fire.

They'd seen us. One man was reaching for their horses, and three of the others were reaching for guns. Only the white-beard remained sitting cross-legged by the fire.

Mike raised his voice in cheerful greeting. "*Asalaam aleikum!*"

The response was the Kalashnikov *clack*—the next was going to be a gunshot.

So they weren't Pakhtuns.

I flattened against my mare's neck and called out in Arabic, "In the name of God, give us water!"

As I spoke, Mike's gelding jumped, then gave a couple of crow-hops. He kept his seat, though, and spoke soothingly until the gelding quieted.

The wind picked up, scattering sand across rock with a sound peculiarly like a stirred fire shooting up a scatter of sparks. One of the tethered horses snorted.

The wind died. In the lull came the resigned voice of a believer. "*Aleikum 'salaam.*"

An older man's voice came from another angle. A third voice translated to English. "In the name of God are you granted shelter, fire, water. But as you value your tongues, keep the holy words out of your infidel mouths."

Mike made a show of motioning Echo and me to dismount and follow him. Oscar...Where was Oscar? His saddle was empty.

Echo leaned his head toward me. "Dude. You totally have to teach me the magic words."

"Later." I know only a few lines in Arabic, and they're all magic. How to pray. How to avoid getting shot. How to bargain for ass.

Regardless of how fervently I might pray, opening that last book of knowledge up here would likely increase our chances of getting shot.

Speaking of ass, where had Oscar gone?

I could guess *when* he'd gone. When Mike's gelding had suddenly and so briefly become an attention-getter.

My mare and I picked our way over broken rock where the rubble was only knee high. Echo followed, towing his mare and Oscar's with his good hand, whistling something that sounded suspiciously like "How Much Is That Doggie in the Window?"

"Shut up, Echo."

Mike solemnly shook hands with every man there, and then I did, and then I took the reins so Echo could. Oscar followed Echo, leaving me holding his horse and wondering exactly when he'd rejoined us.

The western wall was lined with stalls, each big enough for a few men to build a little fire and stretch out around it. The Arabs had the southwest corner, so we took the northwest. Three empty stalls between us wasn't enough for either group to pretend the other wasn't there, but it wasn't space that would protect us. If anything did.

Mike sat on a handy block, his rifle across his knees, pointedly playing the elder statesman role while Echo built a fire. Oscar and I unloaded and brushed down the horses.

By the time we'd finished the horses, Echo was toasting *murghal* spices—cardamom, cinnamon, clove, and pepper—in the bottom of a pot, raising an unexpected and mouthwatering scent in the rapidly chilling air. As Oscar and I washed up, he stirred in a retort pouch of chicken and four of brown rice, crumbled in a mashed-up muffin, and added a squirt-tube of ginger.

Bismillah ir Rahman ir Rahim. I could smell why they put up with Echo. It tasted just as good.

When Echo wiped out the pot and put a cup of water in it, I got the image of him getting his bandage wet and insisted on doing the dishes for him. Any moisture that got in under the edge of that waterproof tape would stay there. His skin was going to macerate enough from sweating through the hot afternoon.

Oscar watched me with an odd expression as I washed the dishes and then spread Echo's bedroll for him. What? Wasn't he used to a doc doing what he could to prevent reinjury? I didn't expect to be coddling Echo after tomorrow, if I did tomorrow, but he needed a little healing time.

I woke before dawn, my muscles as stiff as slabs of jerky, and lay there listening to the Arabs pack up by flashlight. They'd done us no harm, so I wished I could find a prayer in my heart for them. But they belonged here no more than the Americans did. As they quietly left, the height of fellowship I could reach was a sincere hope we never met again, *alhamdulillah*.

I caught a glitter and turned my stiff, aching neck to see a... I guess a visual heaviness, an impression of something man-sized crouching there in the night. The Arabs' flashlights reflected faintly in one eye. He could be Mike or really even Echo. But my money was on Oscar.

With that thought, I went back to sleep.

Chapter Nine

In the morning, I took a moment facing Mecca while Oscar and Mike took turns disassembling and cleaning their weapons. Echo moaned, so I doled out another set of pills to work on the pain and the swelling, but warned him not to take them until he'd eaten enough to buffer his stomach.

He popped them in his mouth instantly, and swallowed with a hearty suck on his water tube.

I glared at him, but I couldn't very well make him unswallow them. I turned to clean my weapon under Oscar's annoyingly close supervision and then watched while he disassembled and cleaned the SAW under Echo's fretful but obviously unneeded directions. I egged Echo on a bit, letting him give Oscar a little more of what Oscar had given me.

I stopped when Mike sighed. "Play *nice*, children."

That might have been my grandfather's voice.

I hurried to pack up my gear and help Echo pack his. The water bladder in his pack was half-full, while mine was nearly empty. I changed them both out, and warned him to drink more.

"We're eating on the road," Mike said and took Echo's reins.

"Whoa, whoa, whoa! With all due respect, sir—Mike—I can eat all by myself. I don't need to be led like some brat on a pony ride at the county fair. Why did you teach me how to steer with my legs if it wasn't to free up my hands?"

Oscar rooted through a pack and unwrapped what looked like a fat Pop-Tart to hand him. "Eat with your left."

Echo giggled. "For two months you've been saying 'Don't use your left hand for anything outside a bathroom. Sit on your left hand if you have to. Stick it in your pocket or under your belt if you have to. Don't use your leyeft, your leyeft! Your unsanitary left! And now you're saying—"

"Don't get caught."

Echo blew a raspberry.

Mike gave me a worried look.

I was wondering myself. Either Echo was taking something I didn't know about, or he was one of those rare people who get completely giddy on a normal dose of codeine. The pills could be tainted, but that was only a remote chance. Especially compared to the chances of voluntary intoxication. Pot, while haraam and shameful to indulge in, was one of the most common summer weeds here. The world's most potent poppy fields were here too. I understood they were kept out of sight now, but I'd bet they were still around.

Breakfast was premade and premashed peanut butter sandwiches, washed down with water from the sippy tubes in our backpack bladders. Chewing got to be a chore, and eating took the first hour of our ride.

Echo announced his second sandwich tasted just exactly like shit.

I asked him how he knew the exact taste of shit.

He flushed and said that wasn't an honest question.

When he finished eating, I retied his shemagh. He rolled his eyes and made kissy noises at me.

"Behave," I said and tapped his nose with my forefinger, expecting to embarrass him.

He laughed and tried to bite me.

Oscar climbed to the ridge, though his helmet didn't break the line of the crest until he'd dropped to his belly to shimmy up the last few feet. He looked over the ridge, back the way we'd come, and in every direction. He shimmied down with the same caution, not standing until he was far enough down that when he stood, I still saw rocks behind his helmet, rather than sky.

"That's a man who knows what he's doing," Echo said and sighed.

I grinned behind my shemagh. "You sound like a man who's been chewed up and spit out for doing it wrong."

"Once. By the walking stereotype there. A'course, I was lucky to survive the once. And the once before, and the once before that."

I shook my head. He was so young. "You never know when your count is up."

"Roger that."

I considered his heartfelt tone and changed the subject. "How old were you when you learned to ride?"

"Everything I did before I came here was sitting on ponies. I thought I was riding, though. I thought I was hot shit."

Behind us, Mike grunted. "You still think you are."

"Nope. Now I know I am."

"Oo rah," I said, mockingly.

He saluted. "How old were you when you learned?"

I lifted one shoulder, a half shrug. "Riding was how we got around. I rode behind my older brother until I was seven. He put me on a horse of my own then so I could help with the herding."

He was staring at me. "You have an *older* brother?"

What could be remarkable about having an older brother? "Why do you ask?"

He glanced back, as if for help.

Mike spoke from behind. "Your records say you're the oldest, Zulu. The one most likely to have a useful grasp of the language and culture. Was someone holding out on us?"

"No." My mare tossed her head, and I laid a hand on her neck. "Hamid died. The Russians shot him."

Echo adjusted his sunglasses. "Soviets, you mean?"

He was such a child. "Same thing, when they're here instead of on the other side of the mountains where they belong. I don't care if they're Russians, Latvians, Lithuanians, Ukranians, Uzbeks, Khazak, Kirgiz, or any of the others. As a group they held half the fucking continent when I was a kid, and they wanted the rest of it."

Mike snorted. "They didn't want the whole continent. They wanted a secure pipeline from the Central Asian oilfields to a warm-water port and decided the best route was through Afghanistan. It was simple economics. They tried to take only what they felt they had to have."

Did Mike think I was as much a child as Echo? That I, the son of Rund the Schoolmaster, didn't know the history of my own people?

"Back when the Brits were strutting around like the baddest bullies on the planet, long before anyone drilled oilfields in Asia, the Russians were throwing their weight around, letting everyone know they were going to move in here as soon as they got around to it. The Brits drew our borders, including that ridiculous panhandle over the north of what's now Pakistan, so they could use the mountains and the Pakhtuns to shield them from the Russians. Meanwhile, the people on the ground, my people, found a national boundary drawn between one brother's house and the next, between a home and the nearest well, between a family's field and its pasture. The Durand Line wasn't designed to divide the Pakhtun, but that's what it did."

"Like the Texas border divided my people," Oscar said quietly, remounting.

"You were warriors and troublesome." Mike admonished. "Even if they didn't draw the line in order to divide you, they had to have been happy with the effect. Divide and conquer. It's quite possible one reason for the line's placement was proclaimed on the world stage, while in private the territorial governors and their military staff rubbed their hands over the real victory."

I didn't know if he was talking to me or to Oscar. Or both of us. Probably me, since he and Oscar both seemed to be trying to change the subject. While I could see the senior team members discussing who should be brought in for the job at hand, having even Echo in on the decision made me feel like an item in a catalog. Trying to distract me from that conclusion was surprisingly considerate of them, but again, the fact every one of them was making an attempt raised questions of its own.

I glanced at Oscar's shape against the rocks ahead. He rode fluidly. I pictured the muscles that would take, the muscles it would build, and had to readjust my jock. Warriors and troublesome, huh? I made a note to Google his tribe, if I could drag the name of it out of my brain.

He'd told me. I remembered the smell of the soap, the welcome hot water, and scraping the hangover nastiness from the surface of my tongue, but I don't remember what he said. Something about the Desert People, but not Navajo.

Echo rode more stiffly and tended to turn his head more than his body when he spoke. "So I guess this Hamid was a lot older than you?"

I blinked. It was summer, so he'd had his birthday. Birthdays…an American notion my mother had brought to the khel. "He'd just turned twelve the week before he was killed."

Echo pointed his masked face at me, centering my reflection in his sunglasses. "It isn't a Russian thing to go around shooting kids."

How many Russians have you polled on the subject? I thought about his bright blue eyes and white-blond hair. "What flavor of Russian are you?"

"The Miami flavor. My dad was born in a Siberian relocation center. My mom's parents came from Kiev; they defected together during a swimming competition. How'd you know?"

I gave my mare a little heel pressure. She lengthened her stride to come abreast of Oscar.

My mother was long dead, but still her honor was mine to cherish. That boy had no need to know how much he looked like my brother Mohammed.

Oscar slanted me what might be the same look Echo had, though it felt different from him. "Need to talk?"

"No."

He nodded, and we rode on.

I'd been nine, not quite ten, the last time Hamid and I rode out with the men. It wasn't my first *lascar*, but the others had amounted to no more than sniping at a caravan of troops or supplies. This was a *daarha*, a true raid on a supply depot just over a day's ride from the khel. And this time, instead of being left behind a ridge or wall to hold the horses, I rode at my brother's side, an ancient bolt-action rifle in my hands and three bullets to shoot. I felt like a man among the men.

We blew up some trucks, stole a quantity of heavy steel boxes along with whatever was in them, and set fire to what must have been fuel and ammunition. It was all noise—overwhelming noise that beat on my skin—and dust and fire and acrid smoke and thrilling terror. None of the Shuravi bullets or shrapnel touched us. We rode away laughing wildly.

We stopped at moonset, only a few hours from home but unwilling to risk the horses in complete darkness. We shoved the boxes into a deep cave, agreeing to check the situation at home first, and return for the booty if no one was watching.

At dawn, while we all faced the southwest and cupped our hands to pray, I saw a mist of a shadow and turned. A pair of helicopters swung out from behind a ridge.

I cried out and jammed myself into a cleft in the rocks. I, the one who climbed to greet the dawn a man's height above my kin, had nevertheless at my uncles' order kept below the ridgeline. That order, and the rocks about me, saved my life as the first helicopter swooped in.

Again, the overwhelming noise battered me, but no thrill zinged through in response. Just numbing terror, the sickening stench of blood and worse, and the noise: hammering bullets, shattering stone, the choppers' motors, and the screams of dying horses, dying men, dying boys.

Then soldiers came. I waited silently, looking down from my dark cleft as they abused the bodies of my kinsmen. By the time the last echoing scream died, I was glad I could no longer tell which was my brother and which was merely a cousin. When the soldiers left, the wild dogs came.

I hid all through that scorching, thirsty day until the kindness of night came to conceal my movement. Then I went home, drank a cup of my grandfather's green tea, and told him how fully one-third of his sons and nephews—and four of his grandsons—had died.

I admitted I had been a coward. I had not called out a true warning. And I had done nothing at all to track those men to their base and spend the final hour of my life wreaking *badal*, blood-vengeance.

He held me close against his thumping heart. He told me a warrior's life is the forging of a perfect blade, that the perfect steel must be quenched as well as heated, folded as well as beaten flat. Sooner or later, inshallah, this badal would come within my daring grasp.

He also told me that while my brother Omar was ready to set aside his childhood, I was now the eldest. Mine now was the burden and privilege to safeguard my *mor*, my mother's honor. Mine now was the duty to forge my brothers' souls, to be as their father and to teach them Pakhtunwali. He would help, but I must set the example.

I swore to him I would.

Then he went to tell his aged father. Kam Ali, my favorite cousin, was sent to tell the women. I sipped more tea and listened to the men speak of redistributing the land and the herds, of who would take on the support of each of the widows and the orphans, while shrieks rose from behind the walls.

"Zulu? Are we going to have problems, you and me?"

I weighed Echo's troubled voice. He didn't sound buzzed any more. I couldn't look at him, not that it would do any good with his face all covered.

If he dropped those sunglasses, I would see my brother's brilliant eyes. I might taste the halwah and apricots my grandfather distributed when Mohammed took his first waddling steps in the courtyard. *Mashallah! A fine boy with my mother's blue eyes!*

What could I say to Echo? *You're fine until you decide to raid a girls' school or mutilate the wounded?* Surely I couldn't be rude enough to even imply he'd do such things. I took a breath and let it out, glad my shemagh covered my face. "No, man. We're good."

Chapter Ten

At lunch, I dismounted like an old man. Half a day in the saddle, and I felt crippled. Oscar didn't insult me with an offer of help, but he hung close. When I wobbled, he just happened to be in the right position to block my butt with his hip and pinch me vertically between himself and his mare. I clung to his saddle for a moment, waiting for the burn in my face to die down.

Echo wanted his bandage off. I let the skin air several minutes, then rewrapped him with just splints and gauze on the promise he'd keep his hand elevated in a sling. He asked for more of the pain pills.

I put three ibuprofen and the last of the Decadron into his mouth. "Swallow."

"I don't get any of the good pills you sign for?"

You weren't supposed to notice that. "Too many doses of that stuff will give you terminal constipation."

Oscar swung back up into his saddle. "Heaven forbid the pretty boy should get his shit chute blocked."

After more than fifteen years at sea, I don't usually react to casual rudeness. Why then did my face feel all stretched and tight?

Mike's voice lashed out. "Shut up, Oscar."

Echo stared wide-eyed at Mike, then Oscar. Then he put his shades back on. At least he kept his trap shut.

Oscar's mare fidgeted. "Point or drag?"

"You've been point all day. Take drag a while."

Mike took point. Echo followed, and I trailed him closely, at his side where possible.

Echo didn't get silly on ibu. At least, no sillier than seemed natural for him. I watched him as carefully as the increasingly narrow, steep trails allowed. He wasn't putting anything else in his mouth unless I saw what it was.

An adverse reaction to a medication wouldn't be a black mark on his record. Whether a tainted batch of painkiller or a marine tripping through a mission on some kind of illicit euphoric, though, I didn't want to have to report any other kind of problem.

I took a couple of ibu myself at the midafternoon stop. Too many years had passed since I'd last spent hours in the saddle. Oscar's jockstrap might be saving my balls from a bruising, but my ass and thighs ached like nothing I could remember. My calves and lower back weren't far behind on the pain scale. Obviously, the exercise machines I'd worked out on didn't cover the same movements as keeping my balance in a saddle.

We were well into the mountains now. The air lacked the muggy heat of Jalalabad, and it smelled of broken stone. Legend says my ancestors once lured an entire army of Ghengis Khan's up into these mountains, then ambushed and slaughtered them. Of all the peoples the Mongols met, we alone weren't crushed. And these clean, hard rocks made up the spine of my history. Despite my burning muscles, my soul sang with the wind.

Heading north and east and north and east again like this must put us right on the Pakistani border. "I hope someone knows where we're going."

"Actually," Mike admitted. "We don't."

My mare stopped dead. I pressed in my heels to urge her on. She didn't move. I loosened the reins, chiding myself to pay attention, and she caught up. "Say again?"

"Our target—call him Tango—went cross-country and probably across the border with our lieutenant. Westerners without Pakistani troop escorts get killed on sight in Khyber province. But these two made it there—wherever *there* was—and most of the way back before Tango disappeared. We suspect Tango went back across the border with the idea he could ask for political asylum and become a *real big man*."

He'd have a real big surprise, especially in the rural areas where Pakhtunwali still dominated the culture. Loyalty was as fundamental to the Pakhtun as it was to the Corps. "So he'd have headed for Islamabad, probably via Pekhawar?"

"Not initially. If they made contacts over there, he'd want to hook up with them to start with, get sanctuary—*nanawatai*—with them. Then go to a big city—Peshawar, probably—only after he has a local family's support and protection."

Go? That's not how nanawatai works. "Pakhtun sanctuary doesn't move around except as the family migrates from its summer lands to its winter lands. If a guest leaves the family's land, the family has no obligation to go with him to protect him."

Especially if they knew he was a traitor to his *qawm*, his chosen companions.

Then again, there was the concept of *bedraga*, escort. Whatever the rules for bedraga were, though, they were not as fundamental as nanawatai.

"Yeah, well. That's one point where we hope your inside knowledge beats his by a wide enough margin to give us a tactical advantage."

Maybe. When I was a teenager trying to remember any of the finer points of Pakhtunwali, I couldn't find much reliable-sounding information. With this war going on and on, there's probably a lot more info getting posted now. But I had given up my research at the same time I'd taken up drinking.

I'd had my last drink. Maybe it was time to take up the research again. "What do you know of his back-up plans?"

"Not much. We had no time to get a subpoena, and the time we might have spent getting a hacker seemed better spent getting you. He'd deleted his Facebook page, but Echo dug up the archives and it had crazy shit. Stop here."

Echo and I stopped. Mike dismounted, climbed some rocks to the right of the road, and scrabbled up to check what was over the coming ridge. In less than a minute, he was remounting. He showed me his phone. "This is him."

I caught only a glimpse of a face, bug-eyed and pointy chinned like a human Chihuahua, before Mike moved ahead on the trail.

"Unless he lied on Facebook, Tango maxed his credit cards and cashed out a trust fund to amass over ten grand. The lieutenant took two grand of his own for emergencies during the trip. If Tango has hired the right bodyguards and hasn't been robbed, he could live well for a long time on the cash. Or he could set up a lucrative business. He supposedly had civilian paramedic training, so he acted as our doc, and twice we caught him telling civilians he was a famous US surgeon doing volunteer work with the military. I could see him teaming up with a translator, setting up a quack medical clinic, and robbing the people blind."

I took a sip of water. This nameless lieutenant had to be one of the boys the major didn't want blamed for Tango's actions. Was he in some brig, incommunicado? Maybe he was being held for ransom? The ransom scenario would explain my presence, but they would have simply explained that to me without all the mystery.

Unless he'd done something nobody should know about, or gone somewhere no NATO was allowed to go. "I take it we're backtracking the two of them?"

"Yes. When we stopped for lunch, that rise Oscar climbed was probably the site of the lieutenant's last call-in."

I hadn't noticed Oscar climbing any rise. Too busy dealing with Echo. "Where does the known part of the trail disappear?"

"It disappeared back there. We circled away from their last camp site, since the area is under surveillance, but from that point we're working on guesses."

I didn't believe him. We'd been cantering every time the ground smoothed out enough to allow it. That was too fast to be going in a wild guess of a direction. "Map?"

He nodded. Echo handed me a GPS showing a topo map. Oscar nudged up behind my mare and handed me the iPad showing what would be a road map if it had a whole lot more or better data.

I juggled reins and electronics, adjusting scale to compare, but there were too many inconsistencies. At least one map had to be inaccurate, and likely both were.

Mike kept talking. "The larger red marks are four towns that are about a day's travel and are big enough to have a horse market. If we stopped at any of them, we could ask whether the lieutenant's mare has shown up. We have good photos of her. The other red marks are two likely villages on the road to Peshawar. The next level of zoom shows smaller villages and khels."

No time to check them all, of course. No time to check any of them, really. If Tango got to Pekhawar, he'd win. "If you're game to cross the border, why not end-run him? Race to Pekhawar and then sweep back along the road to intercept him? Does he have too much of a head start for that?"

"He shouldn't. Depends on how quickly we can move on the other side of the border. Around the next turn there, we should be able to look down on the highway just south of an intersection. The intersection's where we have to make our decision."

Mike scouted the turn, then motioned us to proceed.

I looked at his tired face and wondered if he was maybe a little old for these missions. "I'll take point."

So far, whoever was point had decided our pace. If we were going to head downhill on a steep grade, I wanted the option of taking the descent by foot, leading the horses.

Echo's mare danced, and his bandaged hand came out of its sling long enough to stroke her neck. "No-go, Doc. I mean Zulu. This is what *we* do. My turn for point."

Mike spoke. "Walk it, Echo."

Echo's mare danced again, plainly signaling his irritation. That shemagh might be the only thing between the blond and a charge of insubordination. But after two seconds of hesitation, he obeyed. He was a marine.

Good thing, too. The road down was a steeper grade than before.

I led my mare, letting her pick her footing without my weight to unbalance her. My legs trembled from strain after this long day.

"Halt!" At Oscar's order, I halted instantly. As did Echo.

Oscar slid feetfirst down the scree-covered slope beside the trail, launching miniature avalanches to scatter past us and rain down the cliff to the road below. He stopped to crouch on an outcropping at my knee level. "Funky pothole, eleven o'clock."

I didn't see which pothole in the road beneath us had caught his attention. There were plenty of them. For about fifty yards, the road went wasp-waisted with washouts to both sides...and there, yes, just in front of the narrow place. A repair, rather than a hole. That pothole should have been too small to justify repair given the larger perils left open.

Oscar unslung his rifle, took aim, and fired.

Boom! The explosion below peppered me with rock fragments. My mare shied, her reins yanking my arm.

Boom-Boom-Boom! Boom-Boom-Boom! The explosions shook the ground, stung my skin, stunned my ears. I hit the ground just as the last went off.

A daisy chain. His shot had set off a daisy chain of mines. Probably one designed to have one detonation set off the others. We'd have been hamburger on that road, horse and man together.

Distantly, I heard a yell. A mare bugled.

I turned my head. My mare's hoof came down right in front of my nose, striking a blue-hearted spark against the stone. I squinted to see through the cruelly bright daylight.

Echo was trying, one-handed, to control his panicking mare. She reared, lifting him off his feet.

She came down in slow motion. In slow motion, his boots, his shins, his knees sank below ground level into a cloud bank of rising dust. She'd dropped him off the edge of the cliff. Then she tumbled headfirst after him.

Chapter Eleven

"Halt! Zulu, halt!"

I stopped, trembling with the need to reach Echo. The blond had fallen at least twenty feet, maybe with half a ton of horse landing on top of him. He wasn't even swearing. I saw nothing below but the clouds of dust.

"If it's an active ambush," I said levelly, "y'all take care of it. If it was laid and left, I have a patient to see to."

The dust parted enough to show Echo's mare, shaking her dust-colored head and peeling her lips back from her yellow teeth. But she kept her feet still, holding position like a buzkashi stallion over a downed rider.

"Go to him, then."

The dust moved on the wind, giving visibility by the time I reached bottom with my mare in tow. Echo lay like the tan version of a plastic Green Army Man, tipped over on his back in the dusty road. His mare straddled him protectively.

Something about the barrel and flash suppressor of the SAW, poking out from behind his neck, gave me a cold premonition. "Do not turn your head! Don't move at all."

He didn't speak. Or move. He'd had either the wind knocked out of him or a lick of sense knocked into him. Oh, and his mare stood on the layered ends of his shemagh.

I flopped on my belly and looked under his neck. The assault pack had cushioned his back to some extent, but that protection ended at his shoulders. The SAW's barrel dented his neck heavily where the top of C2, his second cervical vertebra, should have been. If the bone had splintered and cut through his spinal cord, he'd never lift a finger again.

If it hadn't cut the cord, he had a chance—inshallah. I shot a glance down his gig line. An instant, complete severance of the spinal cord gives a man a raging hard-on. His crotch lay flat like any stunned man's.

"Don't move anything, Echo." I spoke to the rising cloud of dust over me and the snipers in it. "Somebody get on the phone and bring in a helo. Tell them to bring a dose of Decadron and a full neck board, backboard. Stat."

I tucked the folds of Echo's shemagh carefully to seal out as much of the cough-inducing dust as possible, then collected the closest dozen fist-sized rocks and snugged them firmly about his neck and shoulders. With that expedient in place, I could improvise more formfitting sandbags to replace the rocks. Had to brace his neck and head for when he inevitably needed to cough or sneeze. A shape approached through the dust. "Bring me socks and an entrenching tool."

"Get on your horse, Zulu." Mike squatted beside me and handed me my sunglasses. "You too, Oscar. We have a mission."

I didn't look at him. "The kid has to be evacuated ASAP. If I get him braced and some steroids in him, and if they get him into surgery before some stray movement manages to cut the spinal cord, he will walk again. He might heal with nothing but a few scars and a stiff neck."

Echo's chest heaved—a good sign, but not as good as it would be if he could still do it in an hour. Sweat freckled his dusty skin with darker spots. "My neck can't be broken. I can wiggle my fingers. All I need is—"

I jabbed a finger at him. "Shut *up*, Echo! All you need is to hold still!" But he was frightened, and snarling at him was ill-bred of me. I moderated my tone. "Combat breathing, son. In three, hold three, out three. Don't hyperventilate."

His chest jerked obediently. That's one thing about a marine: he can obey orders.

I wasn't a marine. I strode to the mares, ripped the Velcro strapping, and threw open the medical pack. I didn't have Decadron, but I had to have something. I just had to figure out what.

"Zulu."

"Shut up, Mike."

"Zarak."

My hands stopped moving. I looked over the saddle into unshaded pale eyes that held no hint of kindness.

"Our target has taken sanctuary with your qawm, your khel."

"Mine." I tried to suss out some kind of code in his words. My qawm consisted of the men and women who handled sick call with me a thousand miles away, especially the few of them who liked to use the gym as often as I did. As for my khel, I'd spent more than three months looking for it the first time, and another war had happened since then. They'd moved, and nobody knew where. What was this game?

I gave it up and went back to analyzing the contents of the med kit.

A hand reached over the saddle and grasped my wrist. "Ask me how I know. *Ask* me."

I glared, knowing he would tell me whether I asked or not. Then I knew without asking. "Ben."

Eyes pale as a desert sky blazed at me. "Tango pestered Bravo no end. Why do these Sunni sing, when those prohibit singing? Why this, how come that? 'I don't know' was never a good enough answer. Two weeks ago, the two of them went on furlough, saying they had a line on finding Bravo's khel. The day they were due back, I got a voice mail. Bravo said they were thirty klicks north of Jalalabad and finally getting more than one bar. Said to expect them by dark. When he was five hours overdue, we went looking. What the dogs had left was mixed with the rags and fluff from his sleeping bag."

Dogs. I couldn't breathe. Dogs don't go for a shot man until he's had time to decompose a bit. To draw dogs within hours, a man would have to be hacked open—or blown open—to expose the dog meat inside.

From hiding, I'd watched wild dogs tear into the remains of my uncles, my cousins, my brother Hamid. Only in my dreams had I gone down from the rocks and slaughtered the scavengers. Only in dreams had I found an undamaged weapon and hunted down the murderers.

Badal. Blood vengeance.

Inhaling, I focused. A target. I needed one, and Mike must have one to offer. "Did the students take them for spies?"

"No. No sign of Tango was left at all, but Bravo was missing only his rifle, his ammo, any money he was carrying, and that Khyber knife you sent him for high school graduation, the one with the Damascus blade. He still had his wallet. Some Talibs might have left that, but any of them would have salvaged the sleeping bag."

The knife I'd had made for him. It meant enough to him that he'd brought it to a war zone, despite the flak he must have taken. "Show me that picture again."

He flipped open his phone, punched one button, and showed me. I stared into the fuzzy copy of a probably outdated picture of the man who'd killed Ben, who'd left him for the dogs. A white man, closer to my age than to Ben's, with a narrow jaw and prominent, angry eyes. The photo shifted to another one, showing the man almost unrecognizable behind an impish grin, then another of him shading his eyes with one hand, looking serious and somehow lost.

Mike snapped shut the phone, then handed me a printout with all three photos and another printout behind it. "Get on your horse and go. We'll call for a helo as soon as you're out of sight. Take all the horses. You can rearrange the packs later."

I pictured the maps in my head, trying to layer the topo and the road map together, and realized I was smudging details, setting myself up for false memories. The map was on the tablet computer. I could refresh myself on the details later. Also, with the extra supplies, we wouldn't need to stop to re-up unless—No!

I had set aside the warrior's way when I chose to be a healer. I knew how to immobilize and transport a wounded man. The people who would come for him probably knew the basics, but I was the expert. I wouldn't risk letting Echo be paralyzed because my ego was so big I had to be on the posse that hunted down Ben's killer. "I'm the doc. I'll stay with him. You two carry on. Bismillah, I can catch up later."

"I can stay with Echo and call for help, or you can stay with Echo and call for help—the result is six of one, half a dozen of the other. But if I went with Oscar to your family, told them the man they were sheltering is a murderer, and demanded that they give him up, what would happen?"

They'd say he could see Tango inshallah, bukhra—tomorrow, if God wills—and delay and delay him until he got disgusted enough to either leave or do something insufferable. Only the father or the brother of a murdered man has the right to penetrate the shield of nanawatai, Pakhtun sanctuary, to demand a murderer be handed over to a *jirga* for trial.

Ben. My pulse pounded in my head. Sorrow. Left for the *dogs!*

Badal, my uncles' voices whispered in my ear. They'd once made a drumbeat of the word, and we'd danced to it: badal, badal, badal.

"Tell him," Oscar growled.

Mike shot him a glare. "We have reason to believe Bravo went into Pakistan. The way things are right now, it would take a foot-high stack of paperwork to allow us to go there. We were hoping you'd find a way to get us through without all that. Should be easy now, with just you and Oscar to move."

Most Momands live on the other side of the border. But how did he think I could convince a Pakistani border patrol I was Momand?

The border patrol might simply accept that I was bent on badal.

"Are we going to jabber all day?" Echo's voice sounded wheezy.

My jaw muscles locked. I swallowed, ripped loose the med kit, and thrust it over the saddle at Mike. "Once you call the helo, poke through here and find something that counts as a steroid. If the helo is delayed at all, pump him full of it. If it's a pill, don't try to let him swallow it. Administer rectally. He can't do anything to raise the risk he might cough, understand? He can't move his head."

The shadow of horses and a rider fell over me. Oscar, waiting. Holding the reins to Echo's mare and Mike's big gelding.

Mike looked past me. "Keep him alive."

"Roger that."

I looked down at the boy. *May God be with you.* I swung up into the saddle, ignoring my creaking joints, and rode north. Oscar followed, his hoofbeats echoing off the rocks with mine. The sooner we were out of sight, the sooner help would be called.

WE PULLED UP in a place where large slabs and mounds of broken rock scattered by some long-ago earthquake offered many nooks and crannies. Oscar scanned the area, then handed me his reins and swung down. "I'll look around."

I tied his reins to an unoccupied D ring on my saddle and watched him. It didn't matter that I could find a sleeping place as well as he could, and would be better at getting away from a frightened shepherd or a huddle of refugees, or even a posse—what we called a lascar—without violence. He'd been assigned to get me safely to the compound, and getting between a marine and what he saw as his duty doesn't get a man anything but trampled.

I scanned the jagged horizon, looking for movement, the wrong silhouette, any sudden glitter, or a trace of smoke. Dry sheep dung made a soft and comforting fire, but it smoked like nobody's business. When I was small, I hated finding a too-fresh dropping that only looked dry from the outside. The fingertips of my left hand stayed raw from being scrubbed clean in the dirt.

Oscar had gone invisible again. I waited, watching, until I saw a movement. The darkness coalesced to form Oscar. He came close and spoke under his breath.

"A group of males, eight or ten maybe, passed this way on foot about an hour ago. They're below us, toward the road. They came from a camp that was used for two nights. Doesn't look like they plan to return to it, though."

I passed him his reins and watched him mount. If they'd gone to check where the mines had gone off or why the helicopter had landed, we'd lucked out in missing them. And they'd likely return to an established camp.

No, if they'd been moving an hour ago, neither the explosions nor the helicopter had drawn them. I had to trust Oscar's sense of timing, which meant the initial movement had nothing to do with us, even if we had influenced it.

Still, he didn't have to actually say *move out*. I let him ride ahead into the darkness. Slowly, carefully. Horses and horsemen don't like the dark.

We stopped again a half mile or so farther north. I took Oscar's reins again, but couldn't see more than the hands that reached them up to me. He melded with the night, became part of it. More Pakhtun in that way than I was.

I examined my resentment and set it aside. With time and close attention, I would learn again what I once had known. Bismillah, with Oscar to teach me, I could master more than I had known there was to learn. *Patience is like its name,* the poet said. *Its taste is bitter. But the result it brings is sweeter than honey.*

"I found a good overhang. You start on the horses while I scout a perimeter."

I nodded and slid from the saddle. An arm caught me. I shoved it away. I was no weakling, to be wobble-legged after a day in the saddle.

Even if my legs had tried to fold under me earlier. The ride hadn't been as long this time. I took care to stretch, though, to make them work. The horses were visible as blank spots, blotting out the stars.

With the horses all hobbled, Oscar vanished again. I pulled my bridle and saddle and set them well under the sheltering rock. The saddlebags followed, both the rustling MOLLE gear and the silent wool local pair. Let all that horse-scented gear draw or repel any scorpions or snakes that might be hiding in my bed-to-be. I checked the hobbles again, feeling my way from hoof to hoof, before setting to with the curry comb. A horseman cannot say alhamdulillah, calling the ride done, until the horses have been cared for.

My father had stood me on a chest-high rock to brush the backs of his prized horses, his father's, and his grandfather's. It was more an honor than a chore, he'd say. I learned every scar on those backs, legs, bellies, flanks, and necks. I learned to seek out thorns, cuts, or swellings that must be lanced.

This mare had been pampered like an American pet, or like the goat-pulling champion she'd be if she were an intact male. Under the coarse hair, bulging muscle framed her spine; hard-muscled legs were cleanly sculpted, works of the breeder's and trainer's art.

I would present her as a gift to my great-grandfather, if he still lived, or to my grandfather.

Unbridling the other three horses took only a moment. I clipped each one's bridle to a D ring on that one's saddle, to simplify the morning's work. The bridles were probably fully interchangeable, but I couldn't tell in the dark, and we might not have time to figure it out in the morning.

The big gelding raised his head, then my mare, then the others. They shifted uneasily, pawing the rocks and testing the lengths of their hobbles. I tried to tune in to whatever they'd heard, or scented, but the high desert night had become too foreign. I wasn't Pakhtun enough to pick out what belonged, or what didn't.

A pack of dogs, maybe. The lions and bears of legend would be long extinct. Wolves, if any were left, counted as dogs.

Wasn't necessarily a danger, either. Sheep or goats wouldn't be a problem. A shepherd would have to be calmed down, but wouldn't be much of a problem if I could speak to him before he shot at us.

If it was a truck, or a convoy, it couldn't get within miles of us. It would have to stop at the washed-out bridge over that last gorge.

A lascar, whether vigilantes, bandits, or Taliban, would be a problem unless they were on a mission that excluded us, or unless they'd already encamped. If they were in camp, Oscar and I could simply approach them and demand hospitality for the night. Arabs didn't have Pakhtunwali, but they had their own code—a demand for water and shelter in the name of God could not be denied. Nor could they stop us from leaving with all our gear in the morning.

If they had honor, that was. But if not, why would they have come here on jihad? I used my feet to jam my horse-load of equipment far up under that slab of rock.

The horses stirred anxiously, pawing the rocks and fidgeting against the hobbles. Whatever was out there wasn't a herbivore. Predator, then, or meat-eating scavenger. I remembered wild dogs attacking our goats and my little brothers, back when I'd had only a stick to fight them off.

Against that memory, the choora I'd bought in Jalalabad felt solid and balanced in my hand. I fished my mare's bridle out of the pile under the rock and slung it over my shoulder. The bit gave it a good swinging weight and it extended my slinging reach by two feet. Such a swing might distract a dog long enough to let me get within knife range.

I nudged the horses to move out, to move downhill toward the trail, away from my rocky nook. Hobbled, they couldn't go too far to be caught again, but if I found myself caught in a knife fight with a pack of wild dogs, I didn't want to be dodging hooves and horse teeth at the same time. Better to catch the dogs between me and their prey.

Having a heavy walking stick would be even better. With a good weighted walking stick, I could brain the fuckers or break their backs. Except those dog attacks years ago proved I had no clue how to use a staff in a fight. Nor had I learned much since then; I don't think watching *Robin Hood* counts as combat training.

The wind carried an ululating hum. Sounded like—I backed under the overhanging rock, trying to catch what I thought I'd heard again. It sounded like— a *dua*? The tongue-twisting Arabic of a prayer? I couldn't tell. I crawled toward the nearest crest overlooking the path.

Whoa—behind—

A weight hit me, shoving me facedown and flat against the rocks, muffling the *thunk* of harness-metal against rock. The scent—Oscar. I didn't need the warning hand clamped over the exposed side of my mouth, pressing a tiny shard into my lip or the tense mass of him to hold down my legs and torso. Fingertips lifted, then tapped my cheekbone, three and three and three. Was he trying to signal an SOS or tell me nine men were coming?

Voices, definitely, speaking Pakhto. At least two had Arabic accents. Shoes scuffled over the rock and cloth ruffled in the night wind. Then silence. I pictured the men noticing the horses and going into combat mode.

I set my mind to ignore the pointed rocks jabbing into my chest and hips, the buckle biting into my armpit, the metal in my ribs. An hour from now, I'd be really lucky to have only such trivia to notice

Someone close by was roundly scolded for spoiling what might have been tracks. He protested that had there been any, no one could see until morning.

At my back, Oscar seemed to relax, settling for a long wait with his head pillowed on the half-empty water bladder in my assault pack, one hand laid possessively over my face, and his heated weight along my ass and thighs. I had to assume his other hand held his weapon, so he could defend us if we were noticed. My knife hilt dug into my hip bone. Anyone who got too close to shoot would be mine.

The horses were brought closer and admired in Pakhto. My guess was they didn't have the delicate lines an Arab would admire. The horses whickered, and one struck sparks from a stone. Loose shoe nail, probably.

My face heated. I should have checked their feet while checking the hobbles. Childishly, I noted that Oscar hadn't checked his mount's feet either. Not that it was my horse, or his, any more. Not unless we managed to shoot nine riflemen in the dark without shooting the horses.

Someone murmured a prayer of thanks for the horses. Shoes scuffed over rock.

Then a nasal voice spoke Pakhto, with a Pakistani accent. "American saddles and gear. Why would those Americans abandon them here, not where the helicopter landed or at the *ziarat?*"

A ziarat—a shrine—was close by. Even if we were captured, they would likely take captives to the shrine. I grinned. We could demand sanctuary there. Once the proper demand was made, the enemy would need apostates with bombs to get us out.

We wouldn't be allowed to keep our weapons or leave, though. That was the downside of ziarat sanctuary.

Some men muttered together in Arabic. At this distance I couldn't make out any of their words.

I stretched cautiously under Oscar. If he'd move so I could I get closer to them, which should be easy enough on this broken ground, I'd be able to pick up some information.

He ground his weight into me. A warning not to move. My Pakhtun soul snarled in defiance, but I wrestled it down. The goal lay north of here, not among this patrol of foreign mujahidin.

Two men checked the horses, but the others stayed between us and them. One of the Arabs whispered the dua for climbing a rise. His silhouette blocked the stars. Standing, at the top of a rise. Visible for... I don't know, but too far. Either he was new at the game or he was confident in his patrol's ability to handle whatever came at them. "Perhaps not all the Americans left in the helicopter."

"Certainly, they did. Look—three with saddles and one spare. At least two Americans left in the helicopter. Do you think a third one hides in the mountains alone? Alone, Abdul? He cannot be such a fool."

Another chimed in. "Where is your faith? We asked for the horses, and here they are."

The one on the ridge raised his hands. "Surely we are provided that which we need, mashallah, but providence often requires that we fight for it as well. Faith and foolishness are not measured—listen!"

Past Oscar's heartbeat, I listened. One of the mujahidin coughed. Beyond that, the wind carried harsh, high noises. Like voices scraping against one another. Not human. A dogfight?

"Dogs! Hear them?"

"Yes! That is what drove the horses so far, despite their hobbles."

"Such thoughts are unworthy. The dogs are merely the tool used to drive these horses to us."

Oscar lay on me, his weight and heat and smell embedding themselves from one side to distract me from the stones digging in from the other.

The mujahidin moved away, arguing in subdued tones. Oscar's hand remained pressed to my mouth. I remained still because he was the one who'd been in-country recently, not because he was on top and I was getting any thrill out of that.

Except I was. And the hot ridge of dick pressed into the back of my thigh said some real interesting things about Oscar.

None of which I could afford to pay attention to right now. The mujahidin would be back at daylight to check for any remaining trail. If we stayed here much longer, dew would form and we'd leave a trail in it. Any minute now, the moon would rise. I supposed a talented tracker could track us by moonlight.

But if they hadn't found the gear I'd stashed, and it sounded like they hadn't, we could at least cut sections of from my other shirt to disguise the tread of our American boots. Without that clue, they wouldn't know for a fact we were worth following even if they did see our tracks.

I tried to shrug Oscar off my back. His fingers clamped harder to my face. More to the point, the dick mashed against my leg lost some of its rigidity. Okay, this was not some domination thing; he had a reason to hold me still. So I held still.

A few minutes later, subtle movement whispered nearby, and an eddy of wind brought the scent of someone who'd eaten curry. A rear scout.

The family's tales spoke of rear scouts, of watching to see what came from hiding after a Soviet patrol or a lascar passed. Once my great-grandfather had scouted behind a British patrol; after it passed, a veiled woman with two small daughters had crept from hiding. He'd taken them home, and the younger girl had eventually married my grandfather.

Oscar held me for a period more, although I couldn't really say if the crawling time amounted to three or four minutes or maybe a quarter hour. Sweat stung my abraded face, and numbness crept in from the extremities.

Finally, he eased his weight to the side. Hot breath found my cheek and ear. "Move out."

Chapter Twelve

I rolled to my back and stretched, disembedding the bridle's buckles and metal rings from my skin, hoping the sounds of my cracking and popping joints didn't carry. When I could trust my feet, I put my mouth to Oscar's ear. "Gear."

He nodded, a scrape of stubble against mine. He had little beard, most of his face being smooth as a Tajik's, but he did have some growth near his jaw hinge and at the chin.

We crawled to the cache, Oscar behind me although I suspected he'd mapped the area in his head and could find it by guess even without my lead. I found the right overhang by scent, horse-sweat in wool. When I made a slight scraping noise, ballistic nylon against stone, a hand touched my wrist, pushed gently. I wasn't sure what he meant, so I scuttled a couple of feet away.

With movement sounds only a lizard might notice, he pulled out what I had cached. He settled the wool saddlebags across my shoulders, atop my pack, then led me across and between and under the rocks, heading downhill most often. He slung the saddle over his own shoulder. That would be a burden, possibly a fatal drag on his energy.

But we couldn't leave it for the lascar to discover when they came back by, or they'd identify us well enough to hunt us down. Too bad we didn't know where the ziarat was. That was the traditional place to stow anything too heavy to travel with.

After my first stumble, I hooked a finger into one of the equipment loops on Oscar's pack, so I could follow him by touch and subliminal cues instead of starlight and guesswork. I held on even after the moon rose, not bothering to justify my actions. Oscar didn't object.

Once in a while, I looked back, checking the toothed horizon and trying to see if we were leaving a trail. I kept looking even though I knew full well that the moonlight wouldn't show me anything. I was doing good to put my feet on the ground without stumbling.

When the dew came, though, if anyone did pick up the trail, we'd be leaving easily identifiable boot treads. I gave the loop a tug, and Oscar stopped. I squatted and touched the rock. Still dry. Not too late to cover our tread. But now that I thought of it, the bandage scissors had gone with Echo. I could cut up the spare shemagh with a knife, but it would ravel and leave its own trail.

I put my mouth to his ear, less to bury my voice than for a chance to breathe his male scent. "Socks over boots. Disguise tread print."

He turned his head and breathed against my ear. "Can you find, no light?"

I'm a sailor. I can find anything in the dark. And the socks were easy. But I just nodded, my beard stubble scraping him. A shiver went down my back, and my dick tried to stand. I eased it sideways before fingering open the correct pouch.

We walked on until the moon was dead overhead and then found a new nook to huddle in. Oscar leaned into the rock with a sigh. "We'll crash here."

Thanks for asking my opinion. I just stretched out beside him, though. "Want some jellied sheep brains?"

"Got some?"

"No," I admitted. So much for getting a rise out of the man. Tiredness settled on me like a blanket.

"What-all did you salvage?"

I pulled a mouthful of water and held it long enough to run through a mental list before swallowing. "My clothes, poncho, liner, a sleeping bag and mat, one bridle, saddle, saddle blanket, and the old-style saddle bag, a sanitary kit, a blister kit, eight meals of halal rations, and a couple more bladders of water." For water, he'd have only what was in his pack's bladder now. He might not have any food. He was Pakhtun enough not to ask for anything until he was hungry enough to munch live lizards. But I was too Pakhtun to wait for him to ask. "You're welcome to anything you want, of course."

"Anything?"

I wondered at the tightness in his voice. But what did he think, that I'd take the sleeping bag and mat and food, and leave him to sleep hungry and thirsty on the poncho? "Anything."

A hand grasped my dick, which surged to life. "I ask again."

Cupping his hand with mine, I held it in place. "This might not be the right time or place to get all naked and sweaty, Oscar."

"Roger that." He didn't withdraw his hand. Instead it massaged, pressing, until I moaned. "Half-naked will do. You need to remove the jock, anyhow. We'll be walking a long way, and that'd chafe."

I didn't think so. It was an excuse, though. I'd said the sensible thing. I'd been reasonable. Now my cock wanted to make the decisions for me, and any excuse was good enough.

I shrugged out of my pack while he opened my pants and shuffled them down my hips, then stopped when they entangled my boots. While I worked my way out of my boots, then stripped off my pants, light whispers of noise, no louder than my suddenly harsh breath, told me Oscar was doing the same. I barely remembered to cap my boots with my socks, to keep unwelcome visitors from climbing in.

The compression straps flipped off the sleeping bag, going somewhere in the dark. I didn't care. A calloused hand gripped my ankle, then ran up my bare leg. I shivered. He yanked the leg straight and dropped his weight on me, trapping one knee bent under my belly.

I grinned and flipped him onto his back. He grunted, but rolled away even as I reached for him. My hands closed on bare rock and a pair of boots.

He knocked out my elbows, folding my arms. I twisted to get aim at him, but he held my arms, twisting them behind me like the wings of a roast chicken. My weight, and his, crashed onto one shoulder and the side of my head. My legs—no—*fuck*—I was pinned but good. My pulse pounded under my skin, and my cock ground into a wad of cloth with an inconveniently placed button.

His hot breath gusted across the back of my neck. "Say uncle."

The fuck I will. "There's ointment for chafing in the bag."

"I got half a mind to do you dry, 'cause you made me work for it."

I clenched my teeth and strained against him. No-go. He hadn't learned his wrestling in a school gym either. "Not if you ever in your life want a chance at round two."

"Can you find that lube one-handed? Count of ten. One. Two."

"Gotta reach the fucking pack!"

"Three."

Only at *three* did he release my left arm. I snatched the bag to me and ripped it open with teeth and hand while he kept my right arm twisted high behind my back and his weight pinning me from the belly down.

"Nine."

"Here, fucker. Here!"

"A man in your position might speak more politely."

I took a ragged breath. "Here, oh wise and wonderful Uncle. Please take it."

A hand caught mine, but instead of taking the packet of ointment, he stroked down my wrist. Then yanked a loop of cord tight at the wrist. I dropped the packet and twisted, heaving, fighting for real this time, trying desperately to dislodge his weight. But his powerful knees clamped in at my flanks, and he released my right wrist only to reveal a tight bracelet of cord on it too.

My balls drew up tight, proving—if nothing else this night had proven it—that they were not the best part of my brain to trust. I saw stars. "Oh, no, you fucker. No you don't. I don't play bondage games."

"You do tonight," he said mildly.

The loops jerked my wrists together, too high to give me any leverage to fight him. He knotted the cords with the backs of my hands touching one another. For a moment he let me test them. "Get your knees on the pad, Zu."

Make me, asshole! I bit back the words right in time. Getting fucked with my knees or my cock on bare rock—even cloth-covered bare rock—would be memorable, but not in the way I liked. "Where is it?"

"Left." He hooked a hand under my shoulder and around my neck, pulling. I got my knees under me on the pad and forced my muscles to relax, hoping to trick him. Once he relaxed too, I could—fuck, do something. Catch him off guard and get to my blade. Cut free. Then find out how much parachute cord I could lay hands on.

But just as I inhaled, ready to shift my balance, an icy drop fell on my shoulder blade. What? Not rain?

Another drop hit my lower spine. Then hard, wet, callus-thickened fingers slid like a letter opener down my crack and bored into my asshole, burning as they stretched and scraped.

No delicate one-finger, two-finger intro here. He shoved in a cold gob of lotion, jabbing in those two stiff fingers and working around. He withdrew them, then jammed them in hard and deep—shoving a grunt out of my mouth—to smear another cold layer.

I pictured him under me, his brown ass clenching around my cock, and then it wasn't any finger. His cock bored in, hard and hot.

I panted, piecing out the pain in bite-size puffs. It had been a long time since I'd had a man that way. Bahrain, I think. Three...four years ago.

I'd been drunk at the time. Drunk enough I might have passed out before the dude finished. No chance of that tonight.

Oscar grunted and reached around to cup my balls. "This would be easier if you'd relax."

It would be a whole lot easier if I was drunk. "You relax when you're tied up?"

He laughed quietly and drove that thing right up my ass.

My prostate spit sparks across my eyes. I gasped.

"Shhh." He released my balls and took a firm grip of my hips. "Rise up a notch."

I obeyed without thinking, shifting around in search of an angle that would make me feel less crammed full. But I *was* crammed full.

As if reading my mind, he eased out, inch after inch. Then he thrust again, jostling my prostate along the way.

Whoa! Yes! But my forehead skidded along the foam pad, thunked against a rock off the end of it.

Oscar dragged me backward to the edge of the mat. "Just lie down, Zu."

So much for a reach-around. But my face wasn't doing too good at supporting the weight of my upper body, especially with those thrusts. So I let him ride me down, his thighs forcing mine wide apart.

His cock felt like it doubled in size. He pulled, dabbed on a little more cold ointment, and thrust deep, grinding feverishly against my prostate while mashing my hard cock into the foam mat.

Oh, that was new. That was good. "More."

"Roger that." He pulled, thrust, ground, really working my ass, reaching deeper inside me than seemed possible, pulled, thrust, ground, setting a rhythm that lit a deliciously hot glow at the base of my balls.

I focused on the glow, on the way his reaming stoked it like bellows stoked the forge fire. Bigger. Hotter. Hotter. He was short-stroking now.

Without warning, the heat blazed through me. I cried out, bucking against the mat.

"Shh."

Took a second to recognize Oscar's hiss. Just then he went rigid, his strong fingers digging into my hips, and hissed again.

I listened to the wind scouring rock with sand and suddenly hoped he was wearing a condom.

He collapsed against me, warm and heavy, a shield against the cold.

My hands weren't caught between my body and his; they were fisted against the mat. I felt the loops, parachute cord all right, cut cleanly between my wrists. I had no idea when he'd cut me free.

One loop shook off. The other fell free when I thumbed the cut knot.

Oscar rolled to the side and made a reassuringly familiar stretched-latex noise. I could all but see him knotting the condom. "Towel, Zu?"

I reached into the pack, fumbling a little, and found the bandannas. Screw Oscar. I needed one to clean myself and the mat and one to keep ready for next time.

Yeah, next time he'd be the one left with a sore ass. Unless one of us got shot before the chance arose.

I pulled on my long johns and pants and wished briefly I still had a clean pair of socks. Or a spare pair. We'd walked the soles out of both my spares. I left my one pair capping my boots. Cold feet tonight would be worth it when I had dry, aired socks for the walk tomorrow.

I spread the sleeping bag. Oscar and I lay atop it, nestled like lovers so that my poncho liner covered us both. And fuck me—why did I feel so good?

Chapter Thirteen

We woke in the first shiver of predawn light, his morning wood against my ass, mine under my hand. I pinched mine down, moved away from his. He grunted and left the hollow we'd sheltered in.

I took the time to wash my face and hands in a cupful of the icy water.

I thought I heard a *shpelai*, the bamboo flute shepherd boys played. From far away, the delicate, haunting sighs might have been the sound of moonlight.

My great-grandfather allowed shepherds to play flutes and sing at night, as the sound seemed to calm the sheep. He forbade flutes in the daytime, or close to the hujra where they might lure a man's thoughts outside the track of obedience. The foolish "children's songs" my mother had taught us in Kabul left him sputtering and chewing his beard. Most of all, we boys could not combine singing and instruments.

Even the *naat*, the women's songs of faith, were allowed to be sung, or played, but not both together. And certainly not where a male might be enticed or distracted from his own observances.

In a city minaret, the muezzin would be patiently holding up two threads, ready to sing out the call to prayer as soon as he could tell the black thread from the white. *La ilaha ilallah.*

I stretched, ears pricked for raised voices in the cold air. None. Prayers don't need vocalization; only men do. But the coming of this dawn called for unsubdued praise. So I raised my own voice for the first time in months. Maybe a year. Maybe more. "La ilaha ilallah."

The echoes mingled one line with the next. "La ilaha ilallah," healing over my clumsy enunciation of the classical Arabic. There's something manifestly *right* about liquid chants flowing over stark rock. "La ilaha ilallah."

When I finished, Oscar scuffed a foot, like knocking on a door, and reentered the hollow.

I bristled, waiting for the snide comment any of my shipmates would have offered. But none came. He simply opened a pack and commenced laying out an inventory of what we had to carry.

I crouched and watched him. I already knew what I'd brought and where it was packed. My control-freak tendencies aren't the jealous kind, though; it doesn't bother me to let other people know all the details too.

Besides, the pause gave me a chance to luxuriate in the peace of the morning. Frost shimmered on the rocks about us, where our breath had collected. The moon rested on a smear of cirrus clouds above the western horizon.

One star hung just outside the horns of the moon. Venus or Jupiter. *El Zohra*, I corrected myself. *El Moshtara*.

On summer nights in Kabul, when I was very small, we'd sleep on the roof instead of in the brick-oven apartment. My older brother Hamid and I would pillow our heads on our father's arms, and he would tell us about the stars, the planets. Years afterward, I realized my father's eyesight was too poor to see what he described so well. How hard had he studied to be able to teach us?

I unfolded the printout with the photos of the man who had killed my little brother. There was another printout with it. More photos.

Two shots of a magnificent gray mare, a classic Arabian beauty. A pixilated zoom-in of her laughing young rider. A group photo, showing the rider between Tango and Mike, with an arm draped around each of them. Oscar stood to Mike's left, with Mike's arm draped over his shoulder and the rider's hand resting on it, but he remained indefinably separate. The four of them wore T-shirts with sweaty dark patches, and their faces shone with sweat. The rifle barrels rising behind them wore condoms to keep the sand out.

Mike and Oscar and my brother. And the man who'd murdered him.

My brother. Ben. Sorrow. My hands shook. I braced my wrists against a frost-rimed stone, waiting for the sun to come up so I could see his face more clearly.

He'd always loved Arabians, always wanted one. I was glad that dream, at least, had come true.

I remember teaching him to shoot, with an old Winchester. My mother had put a stop to the lessons, but not soon enough.

He was born shortly after my father's death, and to my grandparents' distress had been named Sorrow. In the US, he became Benoni, then just Ben. He'd been so mischievous, so full of life and fun.

I'd enlisted when he was what, ten? And seen him only once since then. So yes, I'd abandoned him, but if I hadn't enlisted, the four of us would have been split up. Foster homes could sometimes stretch to accommodate up to three siblings together, but I made four. So we would have been split, two to one home and two to another. Which meant that when I aged out of the system, I would leave one brother alone among the infidels. Without me, the three of them had a chance to stay together.

Sunlight spread around me. Ben had grown up well. His eyes were deep, but not hollow. His teeth were straighter than mine or Omar's. If I'd never had my nose broken, I still wouldn't have those even, balanced features. Some Bollywood actor playing me might look like this man.

My brother.

I folded the page, eventually, and managed to make it slide into my map pocket.

Apart from his rifle and knife, Oscar had a wicked-looking machine pistol. I didn't recognize the style and suspected it was unauthorized. Especially since he hadn't shown it before. His three-day assault pack also held some energy bars, meticulously coiled black rappelling line, and a hank of 550 parachute cord. He had one two-liter water pack that was full and one nearly empty, a jar of iodine pills and a cup filter to purify found water, and a solar ground still—a square of plastic and a cup. That would have been useful last night. It might yet turn out to be useful, depending on what water we could find in the course of the day. He had bullets for the rifle, four magazines for the machine pistol, a pocketknife, two pressure bandages and a packet of blood-stop powder, some camo safety pins, a spare shemagh, and the clothes he was wearing. Everything else was lost with his horse.

"You don't carry your phone on you?"

He shook his head.

"GPS was in your saddlebag?"

He nodded, his lips a straight line across his face.

I had the sudden urge to reassure him. "We know where we are, and we know where we're going. Unless we have to detour around another lascar, all we need to do is follow the map."

He looked over his shoulder, then back at me. "Got a map?"

Well no. The maps had been programmed into the iPad and the GPS. Which the mujahidin took. Which brought another problem front and center. "They'll know where we're going."

"No. If they break the encryption without erasing the data, which isn't a given, they'll find villages marked. They won't know why we're interested or which is our goal. Did the 'din last night say anything to indicate whether they think we're worth ambushing?"

His voice became more animated and less clipped as he spoke. I felt knots in my chest untie in response. "They saw the landing site. The consensus appeared to be that three riders with a spare came by horse, then left by helo, abandoning the horses."

He grunted and measured off a length of the smallest cord. "Pack up. I'll lace the load on you."

In a pig's aye-aye. I pulled myself together and shook out the reflexive anger. He had the rank and the skills. I'd be his pack ass if it let him do what he was good at, because maximizing his prowess maximized my chance of success. "I'll need a quick-release knot."

He twisted a smile at me. I thought he was telling me that was too obvious to need saying. Then I remembered the knots last night and did some of the breathing exercises I'd learned in anger management.

A hand touched my shoulder. I moved away.

The hand hung in midair, then withdrew. "Zu? You okay?"

"In what way do you mean *okay*? Am I scared? No. Injured or sick? No. Am I pissed about being treated like a dancing boy? Yes."

He turned to his own pack. After a moment he spoke as if to one of the coils of line. "You said harder."

Not to him. Not that I remembered. And I'd been dead sober.

His voice roughened. "You only take it from officers? Or only from white men?"

It took a moment. Then I remembered the blond in Jalalabad. I laughed. "That guy with the mustache was an officer? *He* said harder."

Capable hands hesitated. Then they stroked the lines, nestling one coil inside the other.

I felt them stroking me, just as capably. I shivered.

"I guess I owe you one, Zu."

I thought of touching his shoulder, but he might move away. As I had. So I put it in words. "I'll take you up on that."

Chapter Fourteen

At first, Oscar was difficult to keep up with, but it got easier when I set my own pace, marching under my load, and let him range about checking for oddities or movement to either side, ahead, and sometimes behind. Looking up was strictly his job. I had to stop and cut a thorn tree to make a walking staff.

The road was deeply cratered in several places, and when we moved through a valley where I could see side to side, I saw the fields were deeply cratered too. The number of weeds indicated the ground was fertile but left fallow. The craters were too steep-sided to plow.

How hard would it be to helo in a little earthmover to level out the ground, move the stones aside, make this field fit to plow again? The army had the equipment. They might do it for the good PR. I'd heard the arguments about giving people something to lose.

People with nothing to lose are ripe for any extremist who claims to have answers. People who claw a living out of sand and stone don't readily give it up to go join a jihad, but there has to be an *it* to give up.

Oh, but the hollow-eyed students with their burning souls would notice the feranghi cleaning up one field. They'd bring a lascar through to burn the crops and everything in the houses. The shunnings and beatings would follow, until the farmers gave up and left. Then the nicely leveled field would become the property of the strongest bully in the area.

But what if someone came through along a straight line, like Sherman's line to the sea, only instead of destruction they leveled all the craters and rubble piles that were visible from the sky? Then this would be just one of hundreds, maybe thousands, of leveled fields.

Anyone who wanted to do that needed to do it now, before the spring planting.

Close to noon, we reached a village. The women at the well covered their faces, and, after quiet discussion among themselves, moved aside so we could drink. It was a hospitable gesture, but we couldn't very well say thank-you to women we didn't know. Oscar solved the problem by saying "Dera manana" to a snot-nosed toddler clinging to one woman's skirts.

Oscar's filtration cup turned out to work better than I'd expected. I was just as happy to sit on a pile of rubble that had been someone's front wall, resting my shoulders and back, staring at the sky. When I stood and stretched, Oscar gestured me to leave the load where it was. He watched it while I explored this place's miserable excuse for a bazaar.

We'd missed the horse market by several days, naturally. I bought broiled pumpkin kebabs from a pair of boys in colorfully embroidered caps. They looked bored and very happy to strike up a conversation with a traveler.

After paying, I asked if this was where "those buzkashi stallions" had been bred. For a reasonable fee, the boys eagerly described an outlying khel that produced very strong stock—without a doubt the chapandaz-quality stallions we had heard of. For a reasonable fee, they could give us directions. One of their cousins even had a truck that could take us there—for a reasonable fee—to ensure we arrived well rested and without getting lost.

I'd about reached my limit of tolerance for the shakedown. I was about to ask if we'd be charged a reasonable fee for the truck, a separate reasonable fee for the driver, and a third fee for the petrol, but Oscar's chuckle reined me in short.

The horse-breeding khel didn't seem to have electricity, but there had to be a generator or a solar cell in there to power a phone, because they sure knew we were coming. They mobbed the road to greet us and practically dragged us to the corral where three fine colts and one that looked extraordinary danced. They asked only the price of a new car for the best two, which were partially trained.

I admired them while Oscar selected a pair of sturdy fillies, too young to be valuable as breeders and only green broke, but with short, thick-muscled backs and heavy leg bones. They cost a full magazine apiece, along with all of Oscar's rupees and euros. I got the filly that the saddle fit, while Oscar got a worn-out local saddle. Then we headed east again, seeking a pass we could use to get across the border.

Dusk thickened in the valley, though I could look up and see afternoon in the sky and on the snowy mountain peaks. When I looked down again, the dusk around me seemed denser. Ah, I'd ruined my night vision by looking into the brightness overhead. I said my evening prayer and kept my eyes down.

When the sun left the sky, we rode on in the dark. Now I could look up, watching the stars shimmer into place and the planets appear, ready to lead the moon in the track ordained for them. In another month, the fireflies would fill these valleys with tiny floating candles, but then the mosquitoes would outnumber them.

At moonrise, Oscar headed downhill off the road.

I dismounted to lead my filly. She might be good at walking downhill in the dark with a man on her back, even on rough ground, but that wasn't something to count on. And why had we left the trail?

He came back in view. "We'll keep the horses between us and the road, to confuse any echoes."

"What have you found?" Was there a cave, or a good overhang, or a tight opening between the rocks to hide and sleep in?

"A good place to fuck."

My blood pressure surged. But no-go, no-go. "We have nothing for lubrication."

He disappeared into the darkness. "So?"

I blinked. Anger stirred, like fire catching on the tinder of that harsh voice. "Are you used to taking it dry?"

Did he know how much damage he could do himself like that? How much the abrasion increased his chances of catching any passing infection?

And if he thought I was taking it dry, we were going to match blades first.

I followed him into an enclosure, partly raw stone and partly brick, but roofless so that the moon dimly revealed piles of rubble all about. A plastic bucket that didn't feel cracked had been wedged into the bricks near the doorway. I hobbled my filly next to his, poured a test cupful of water into the bucket, and shared a silent moment removing the tack and running our hands over their legs, inside their hooves, and along their backs, checking for any chafe or injury.

I kept hip-nudging the fillies away from the water, but finally checked and found still about the same amount in the bucket. I poured in about a pint more—not enough to satisfy even one horse, but I could refill it more easily than I could deal with wasting water.

After a moment, I noticed Oscar's mare was standing alone, peacefully slurping at the water. I turned and found him sitting naked in the moonlight. Watching me.

"Ain't used to taking it any way," he said.

Before I could say, *then don't*, he hunched down, planting his elbows on what I realized was an unrolled fleece or mat and resting his forehead in his hands, completely submissive.

That quiet admission took all the remaining anger out of me.

I undressed and knelt behind him, admiring the subtle sheen of moonlight on his skin. Then I realized it meant he'd broken a sweat.

I pulled my knife and slid it across his flank like a razor, feeling the initial smoothness and then the chill bumps rising, trying to catch the edge of the blade.

Angling the edge back, I swept it over his skin without risk of cutting in. Units that kept their soldiers in the field longer than overnight were routinely allowing them to grow beards because a break in the skin, however shallow, is risky in a foreign land. But how foreign was this land to a man like Oscar?

I lifted the blade, turned it to catch moonlight on the ribbon of sweat scraped from his skin, and tasted it. Dust and salt and musk. Essence of Oscar. I smeared it over my cheek, the cold steel raising my own chill bumps, and scraped up another load of sweat to wipe over my other cheek. Painting my face with Oscar.

Nobody else would ever know I had done this. But I knew.

Oscar didn't move. He had to be wondering what I was doing, but his discipline—or his pride—held him still.

A warrior, given to me to use or abuse as I saw fit.

I drew the blade tip down alongside his spine, pulling a dark matte streak of dry skin in the moonlit shimmer of sweat. Just a little more pressure, a slightly different angle, and that would be a blood streak. He wouldn't object. He wouldn't let himself.

Again I tasted the blade, the salt and the skin oil and the man. The man who shivered against my thighs.

I folded down over him, shielding him from the sharpening wind, and resting my weight on his powerful back, his powerful legs folded beneath him. I sniffed behind his ear, down his neck to the shoulder, the warm amberlike scent hardening my cock against the small of his back.

I set the knife aside to reach between his knee and elbow and found his cock against his belly. With fingertips on it, I flicked my tongue against his ear. His cock lunged against my palm, hardening further as I grasped it.

Still, he made no sound. No protest, of course. What was I trying for, begging? No. Something in me recoiled at the very thought.

I took the blade into that cave he'd made of his body, pressed its cold length against his belly. He tensed. Couldn't really call that a flinch. I scraped the unsharpened back of it quickly across his nipple.

That brought a flinch and a growl. Quickly swallowed. But no move to protect himself.

I set the knife aside again and moved sideways, knee-walking steps, so I could balance with my left hand on the stone beside the mat, and with my right reach in and cup those warm heavy balls. They moved, as if exploring my palm.

I released them and grasped his cock, now clear of the delicate sheath of foreskin. He thrust into my grip.

I could have his ass. Because I could, I didn't need to. Taking him that way would prove nothing, except perhaps that I had a petty sense of vengeance.

Vengeance is too powerful to waste on a man's honest mistake. I thrust against his sweat-slick back, humping him like a teenager with my cock clasped warmly between my body and his, sliding against his skin. My cock didn't need the grip of his ass.

The revelation exalted me. I didn't need him to pay in pain.

He thrust too, fiercely fucking my hand. The sweat gave out, was replaced by a smear of precum and then more sweat, mine and his together. Still we shoved at one another, clenching our muscles and fighting as if to break through barriers of skin and self to each merge with the other. We struggled together to reach that brief foretaste of paradise.

Our gasps echoed against the stone and brick walls. Something hard in the fleece beneath us dug into my shin, but wasn't worth moving.

I got there.

Light burned through me, scorched from deep in my ass through my balls through my cock, turning into pure wet heat shooting out across Oscar's back.

Oscar laughed soundlessly under me. I fell onto his back and laughed with him. But he hadn't made it yet.

I cupped his balls again, explored the loose skin that made him hiss. When I moved to the side, I had to unstick the cum that glued us together.

But he was losing rigidity. What he needed wasn't a soft-handed exploration. I balanced across his back and pumped his cock with one hand, cupping his balls and mashing my thumb hard on the puckered line leading back from there.

A man jerking himself off has a better effect than a man trying to tickle himself, but someone else can still do a whole lot better. I caught a thatch of his hair in my teeth, pulling hard enough to add a strain to his harsh gasping breath. I fell into rhythm with it, pulling in time to my pumping hand.

He groaned out a deep, rending sound like an oak twisting its roots free of the earth, and spasmed in my grip. I held him as he bucked under me, keeping my grip on his cock with difficulty.

He collapsed slowly into the sheepskins. I guided him down.

"Fuck," he whispered, sounding dazed.

I smiled in the darkness. This time I let him clean up with my shemagh. I cleaned up with the same one, then knotted it to remind myself it needed washing and tucked it in the corner of my pack. "Let's pick up some lube at the next stop."

"Roger that."

Chapter Fifteen

The next morning, the booming of a waterfall brought us to an icy stream plunging into a gorge so deep no daylight lit its depths. Oscar found a mud basin near the fall and patched it with clay and rocks. I used his plastic sheet to divert a splashing stream to fill the basin so the horses could drink. While they drank, we rinsed and wrung our socks and underwear repeatedly in the painfully cold falling water, sponge-bathed with the clean cloth, and rinsed them many more times. My hands ached.

I mumbled something about not really having the time to stretch things over rocks to dry. Oscar showed me how to clip them to our packs to dry in the wind. My red and aching hands were too clumsy to operate a safety pin by then, but he just grinned and pinned my socks for me.

We caught more water, filtered it, and refilled the flattened bladders in our packs.

The wind picked back up. I stood shivering in the lee of my horse, breathing her dusty, warm scent, while Oscar cleared the signs of our stop. My hands were brilliant red, and my sleeves were wet to the armpits.

"We need to sanitize our packs," I said when he'd finished.

He rolled his sleeves back down over his muscled forearms. "Cache it here? Wouldn't that be obvious?"

I shivered and thought longingly of hot food. As much as I'd sweated through the afternoon, that cold water and the chilling wind had sucked all the living heat out of me. "There'll be a shrine nearby. There's always a shrine. Anything left there will be sacrosanct until we return for it."

He looked at me, then seemed to focus his attention on the complex and mentally taxing puzzle of how to button his cuffs. "I think you're talking about how things should be. Or used to be."

Of course. What else did I have? "Wasn't the whole point of your bringing me on this mission to use my memories of how things used to work, how they're supposed to work?"

"Mike's an optimist."

What answer did I have to that? But it didn't matter, since we didn't find a shrine.

At the next crossroads, we approached a man loaded like a donkey, trudging three-legged with much of his weight on a knotted staff. He looked so worn by work and hunger I couldn't guess his age, except to hope he was older than me. When we came close enough to smell him, the bundle moved. I reined in, startled.

The bundle he carried was a woman. Her frighteningly thin hand drew a fold of cloth over her haggard face.

I swallowed. The standard greeting, *may you not grow tired*, would be obscenely ironic here. I touched my forehead. "Asalaam aleikum, Uncle!"

"*Wa alaikuma as-salaam.*" He leaned on his staff, his breath coming in wheezes and sweat beading all over his face. Sweat crusted his gray *shamiz* too, making a camo pattern of whitish salt, dun dust, and gray fabric. Even his beard too was gray and white and dusty. "Have you seen the nurse-officer?"

I wasn't entirely sure I understood him. I shook my head, though, because we hadn't seen any females who seemed likely to fit such an unusual description.

He leaned harder on his staff, mumbling to himself, then raised his anguished eyes to me. "Tell me please, she has not moved on again before we have reached her?"

"I do not know. We came to a village only to buy horses and saw no extraordinary females there."

"No crowd? Then she was not there." He looked eastward. "This way, then, is my road. May you not grow tired." He trudged uphill.

I couldn't stand it. I swung down. "Please! I am tired from riding, but this foolish horse needs more work to teach her patience. Could you do me the favor of riding for the next little distance?"

He blinked many times. Tears beaded his eyes and rolled down his face with the sweat. "You are truly Pakhtun. So rare, in these hard days."

Me? No. I was just human and trying to hold on to my humanity.

He tried to mount, but the weight on his back was too much. Nor could I give a quick boost without shaming myself and them.

But I'd positioned uncooperative bodies before. He had one of those serapelike blankets poor people wear when they can't afford a coat. Oscar and I could use that as a sling to lift the woman. Okay, the trick here was that I didn't know how to mention the woman without offense.

So...okay. Don't mention her directly. "If you should spread your blanket on the ground, Uncle, someone could sit on the blanket. If you should then mount the horse, my man and I could lift the blanket up to you."

He finger-combed his beard and agreed this might work very well.

For a while the trail was wide enough I could walk at his stirrup, using his staff to push past thorns that crowded me. And sort of just staying handy in case the woman perched behind his saddle should fall.

The man chattered, whether from pure relief or what I don't know. His name was Khiel Khan.

I gave my name as Zarak only, because I wanted him to keep talking. I was Momand, while his name said his ancestors had likely been clanless Punjabi Muslims who'd fled India after Partition to escape the Hindi mobs. He asked about my family. I thought about lying, but instead asked about his. He nodded sagely and changed the subject.

He'd carried his wife from their khel to a village where the traveling nurse-officer was set up with her... These weren't words I knew. From context, he might mean a clinic. He'd risen well before daylight to reach the...something...before she left that village, but had stood aside from the road, averting his eyes, as a truckload of women drove by, an armed guard perched on their front bumper.

"I saw her go," he kept saying, mournfully. "But I did not know one of those women was the one I sought. What honorable man looks at unknown women?"

He cupped his hands and studied them, as if praying. Then shrugged. "I saw her go."

He'd followed them to the next village, knowing the pattern was to spend two days and expecting his own trip to last one day. But the nurses had been threatened and had left the same day they arrived. He had become desperate, and God had brought him us. "As fast as a young man can walk with your little pack, bismillah, we will intercept them very soon!"

His wife murmured faintly. He lost his enthusiasm and groped in a pocket. Handing back a smooth pebble, he advised her to hold it in her mouth to ease the thirst.

As sick as she seemed, as thin as she was, dehydration would kill her as quickly as anything. I shrugged out of my pack and fished out the still-sealed bladder of water. "If you thirst, Uncle, drink of this."

Again he blessed me, with my fathers and sons for many generations. He unwrapped the sealed nipple and tasted the water, then handed the nipple back to his wife. "But you have been bold, brother! This is of English make!"

"An American gave it to me."

"English, French, American? They are all the same when they come to Pakhtun lands: foreigners!" He spit. "Infidels! You should not take gifts from the devil's men, oh my brother, for they will demand your soul in payment."

Speaking of payment, brother, it's time to pay for the ride. I unfolded my printout to show Ben's mare. "In your travels, have you seen this horse?"

"No, I have not been blessed to see her with these eyes. She is said to dance like a horse of the paryan, though!"

I didn't look at Oscar. He was either catching this or he wasn't. "What else have you heard said of her?"

"They say she would make a mullah dream of daarha—just one raid, to steal so fine a mare. Surely a holy man's soul could bear the price of one raid."

"It would depend on his age and health, would it not?"

He laughed too heartily, as if he hadn't had a good reason to laugh in way too long, and as if he was running the thin edge of hysteria. A painfully thin hand reached from under the burqa and touched his cheek. He leaned into it.

When it withdrew, he looked at me soberly. "My cousin's cousin saw two men ride from across the line. Their guide was thought to be wicked, or stupid, for the road here is very bad. The tall man, who had a rifle as fine as this mare, as fine perhaps as your man's, rode the mare on this very road, and some days later rode her back across the line into Afghanistan."

He took another pull of water, then handed the drinking tube back to his wife. "The tall one was a mystery, and so he caused much talk. Is he Pakhtun? Why does he sound so odd if he is? Why does he look so familiar if he is not? With him rode a cigar-smoking kafir on a dun mare. They came together; they went back together. Then, two or three days later, the kafir returned, with both horses and both rifles, and no companion."

"What road did they take?"

He shrugged elaborately. "A man who carries no gun is wise to notice very little about the well armed."

But he'd noticed plenty and shared it freely. Taking chances. *Dera manana, oh my brother.*

He lapsed into silence. The trail rose steeply. I held on to the stirrup for support and let the horse pull me up the trail. And I let Khiel Khan stew in his qualms, while every stride built his debt to us.

When the trail narrowed, Oscar pulled up and dismounted, waving me to catch up and the other rider to pass. Then he jerked his head, and I took it as a signal to mount. He wasn't wheezing in the thin, cold air. I was, so I took his horse. As I did, he slid ahead of the one Khiel rode and led the way up the trail on foot.

I would have liked to ride directly behind him, watching that glorious body at work, but sandwiching Khiel between us was smarter.

After about an hour, Khiel looked back at me over his wife's head. "Is your man at least a man of the book?"

"He is." I hadn't asked, but it was a pretty safe bet. I would have liked to know how he'd deduced Oscar was no Muslim. The deduction put Oscar in peril and went naturally with others too dangerous to confirm or deny.

Oscar raised his hand, and the parade stopped instantly, silently. He trotted forward in a crouch, rock to rock, studying something I couldn't see past the double-loaded horse between us. He came back and spoke in his rough Dari. "Village ahead. Friendly?"

I translated to Pakhtun. Khiel looked woebegone. "Alas, not for you, even if the Momand themselves were to protect you. I will walk from here, bismillah, and will find the nurse-officer."

Inshallah. He didn't have to say it out loud.

He dismounted and looked up at me. "If a man were so bold as to follow the hoofmarks of the kafir, he would ride back along this road. Perhaps half a kilometer before the intersection where we met, a thorn-cursed track splits off to the south. After a few kilometers, it turns west to the border, then sharply back east through a pass to a cart road that leads to the road to Peshawar."

He went back to the mare he'd ridden and turned his back to the saddle. His wife climbed down onto his back. He seemed much restored by the rest and the water. When he tried to hand me back the limp bladder, I insisted he keep it.

His face twisted. Oh, maybe it wasn't safe for him to carry NATO equipment?

I capped the bladder, which had a pint or so left, and set it in my pack. Oscar took my mare while I kept his. That put the heavier rider on the more fatigued horse, but the thirty pounds or so he topped me by ought not be enough to make a difference.

Chapter Sixteen

We retraced our way to the intersection, found the thorn-cursed track, which did wind back to a view of the single strand of concertina wire that marked the border here. But someone had paved the road east from there. Or either we were lost.

Oscar told me marines are never lost. Just occasionally misoriented.

I looked at the thorns and the rocks. This would make excellent ambush country.

Oscar dropped his mare's pace to a walk. "We're surrounded."

"We would have been sooner or later. Keep your hands off your weapons."

"D'uh."

I reined in and lifted my voice in Pakhto. "Are you lascar, soldiers, or bandits? Show yourselves, if you please."

A man in mirrored shades and sharply creased camo uniform stood, apparently from behind a pebble. "The question, sharp eyes, is who might you be?"

There was absolutely no way a bandit would be wearing that spiffy uniform with that insignia. The Frontier Force would roast him alive, slowly. I wished I could recognize what rank his buttons showed. Officer, certainly.

I raised my hands carefully, pushed back my shemagh, and flipped my sunglasses to fall to my chest. "My grandfather's father is Zarak called Hajji. My grandfather is Mohammed, called the Wise. My father was Abdul Momand, called Rund, who taught at the university in Kabul before the Shuravi came. My name is Zarak Momand also, and this is my follower."

He moved his face slightly toward Oscar, before aiming those mirrored shades back at me. "What has driven you to cross the line precisely midway between authorized crossing posts?"

I spread my hands. "Are we not Pakhtun? What is this line to us? I will have badal of a stranger among you, but to your people I am no aggressor. Surely, the Book says, 'God loveth not those who are aggressors.'"

As I spoke, a young man with the double chevron of a *naik*, a corporal, whispered to a bearded *havildar*. The havildar approached Mr. Spiff and saluted. They spoke a moment.

The officer smiled tightly under those mirrored shades. "The line is real enough, and any who cross it without permission might be considered aggressors. Please, dismount and hand over your weapons."

He lifted one hand carefully, and young men in rather less spiffy uniforms unfolded themselves from behind various rocks and shadows of rocks. Each carried an automatic assault weapon, of a type I didn't recognize.

I kept my hands clear of my belt. "We are not smugglers. You may search the baggage. We have neither goods nor money to buy them."

"Thank you so much for giving permission. Dismount, please. And disarm. I will not ask a third time."

So we were out of options. I pegged him as a senior lieutenant or a young captain. He was too old to be a second lieutenant.

Something about him gave me the feeling he'd risen as high as he ever would. I'd watched enough men like him—and their victims—to know that the first hint of disrespect would have him extruding fangs and striking out, even if doing so might harm what remained of his own career. So I schooled my face to extreme respect.

I had no way to know how much of that conversation Oscar had followed, but he was alert enough to take a cue from my face.

A hard-faced boy with no rank on his sleeve approached warily and grasped my mare's bridle. I unslung my weapon and handed it down to a second boy, who was just as hard-faced. Then I dismounted, as gracefully as I could with all those people watching me.

Oscar's mare fidgeted. The tendons on the backs of his hands stood out like cable.

"This is my follower," I said firmly. I was claiming him, so that even if he was seen as kafir, no man could touch him without expecting a Pakhtun to defend or avenge him. But for that protection to hold, he had to obey me. I went to touch his rein and looked up, willing him to give in.

Oscar reached down to hand me his pistol and then, reluctantly, his rifle. Finally, he dismounted.

I passed his weapons to the boy who held mine. Oscar was saying he held me responsible for that rifle, I knew. Those things are customized to each sniper; replacing it would take months once the paperwork went through, assuming the paperwork went through.

If he was chief level, he might not be issued a new rifle. He might be stuck behind a desk for the rest of his career.

We had to get out of this alive and without causing an international incident, before we needed to worry about either of our careers.

Besides, we both still had our knives.

"Knives, sir," the boy said.

I untied my sash and wrapped both my choora and Oscar's KA-BAR in it.

The boy went to the officer, who immediately selected Oscar's rifle out of the armload. "A fine weapon."

If a guest in my home admired it, I'd have to offer it as a gift. Not rushing to offer it now might be rude. I chose a cautious rudeness. "Fine indeed. It was made for my man and is irreplaceable."

"Identification, sirs?"

"I regret, sir, we carry nothing but the means to find our quarry and bring him to the jirga for trial."

He looked at me and at Oscar beside me. "Show me what you have."

I unfolded the first sheet of photos. "This is him we seek." I passed the second without unfolding it. "This is my brother and his qawm."

The officer slung Oscar's rifle, as if trying it on for size, and studied the photos. "The young one favors you strongly. All his chosen companions are foreigners, but for himself?"

"Yes, sir."

"Please, turn to face the sun."

I took Oscar's shoulder and turned him, before turning myself.

The officer studied Oscar's sunlit face. "So you also were one of his qawm?"

Oscar looked at me.

The officer slashed the back of his left hand across Oscar's mouth.

Don't react, Oscar! I launched myself between them, hands wide like a basketball guard. "This one is mine to discipline, sir! And mine to protect!"

The officer smiled faintly at him, not at me. "I see."

I didn't ask what he saw.

He unslung Oscar's rifle and laid it back in the boy's arms. "Your belongings will be returned if you are vouched for."

By whom? If he was working with NATO troops, they'd immediately ask for our ID. Or at least Oscar's, since he'd be undeniably American to anyone who heard his voice or saw that rifle.

We walked through a narrow draw to a twisting trail up to a shed surrounded by motor scooters. The shed was roofed with solar cells and spiked with radio antennas. The bearded havildar unlocked the shed and brought out a cell phone. He handed it to the corporal who'd whispered earlier.

Oscar and I stood with our backs to the sun. Our pockets were emptied, but they didn't knock us around to do it. Our saddles and meager packs were unpacked and dismantled, but not wrecked or scattered. My seeds—beans, lentils, pumpkin, okra, sunflowers, and things I didn't recognize offhand—were examined with much curiosity, but rewrapped with rather more care than anything else got.

After examining everything, they shoveled it all into my pack.

A truck came. We were loaded into the back of it with one young guard, while the officer rode in the cab with our weapons. I looked back at our mares and saddles. For what they'd cost per mile we'd ridden them, that was a pretty poor return on investment.

The truck turned onto a dirt road and picked up speed. I sat on the bed—or tried. It was rather like sitting on a trampoline while an Olympic hopeful bounced himself and me. The young one-striper with the short-bodied machine gun clung to the gun mount on the back of the cab, his feet leaving the bed of the truck about as often as my butt did.

Oscar crouched beside me, using his powerful legs as shock absorbers, one hand on my shoulder and the other on the side of the truck. He seemed to be memorizing the route until the dust rose too thick to see more than the angle of the sun and one glittering mountain peak that mostly stayed on our left

A herd of shaggy donkeys loaded with burlap-wrapped bundles scattered on both sides and yee-hawed plaintively in the dust cloud we left them. I've never been able to figure out how the little beasts could be so heavily laden. These certainly were dwarfed by their burdens. Yet all remained nimble enough to avoid getting tagged by a bumper.

Or maybe one had been tagged and was just invisible in the dust. They were pretty much the color of the dust and the road and the burlap.

The truck swerved to the right, hard, and stopped hard enough to throw me into the machine gunner, and Oscar into me.

A voice called through the dust. "Welcome many times! Our home is honored to receive you, sir!"

Oscar turned his masked face to me. I shrugged. I didn't think they were talking to us. We stood and dusted off anyway. If we were invited inside, it wouldn't be polite to carry half the road in with us.

A scrawny tree emerged from the settling dust. It was just budding out, some of the buds swollen enough to show tiny tongues of pale blossom ready to emerge. Passing it, Oscar cupped one of the delicate blossoms in his thick-fingered hand. He paused to study it, then moved on without a word.

We were indeed invited in. It looked like the living room of a private home, with pale blue walls and wicker chests lining one wall, and a carved wooden room divider hiding all but the top arch of an interior doorway. They'd spread a heavy golden carpet with a pomegranate design woven into what would be the red squares if it were a giant checkerboard. Plush and unmarked, it looked like no foot had ever set on it, much less field boots like ours.

I folded my legs to sit near the edge closest to the door, with Oscar close beside me. Might as well be modest instead of claiming too high a place and be scorned for arrogance. The driver stood off the carpet behind us, plainly on guard. The officer took a proffered footstool half facing us. The corporal sat facing him, claiming a higher social rank than Oscar and me, but not by much.

We all shook hands with a nervous man in a checkered turban and a navy blazer over a tightly buttoned western-style gray silk vest.

An elderly servant brought a tea tray of dark wood, elegantly carved, with polished brass handles that matched the carpet. He tiptoed across the carpet to place it in the exact center, then scuttled away.

The nervous man poured tea and served white cubes of *halwah*. The tea had enough sugar to taste like heated syrup. The halwah was even sweeter. The nervous man raised his cup. "Long life and happiness."

The officer raised his. "Peace and wealth to your house."

"Peace and happiness to the guests," offered the corporal.

My turn? I touched my heart to show sincerity. "Safety and peace to this house and all herein."

I hoped Oscar took his cue. Beside me, he spoke in English. "Live long and prosper."

I choked on my tea. Oscar thumped me helpfully on the back.

A door opened behind the divider. From behind it, with some bustle and a brief whispered exchange, came an older man who seemed to have dyed his beard with black ink. His very bushy eyebrows remained white, like fuzzy caterpillars over his eyes. The nervous man brought him a footstool, set it in the host's place facing the door, and thanked him effusively for coming home so soon. We all stood and shook hands with him too, reiterated the round of good wishes, then resumed our places on the carpet.

The old man had carried in the scent of fried food. With the sweet stuff sitting unaccompanied in my stomach and the smell of mutton fat that wouldn't go away, that added scent was nauseating. I told myself the tea would settle me, and I sipped it determinedly.

The officer and the old man expressed mutual delight and honor in meeting one another, then explored the possibility that the old man's brother had attended school with the officer's father. They concluded, regretfully, that no such connection existed.

More tea was poured and slowly consumed. Or I made a point of consuming it slowly. It's not like I could politely ask to use the bathroom if I filled my bladder with tea.

Perhaps an hour oozed by. At about the same rate, pins and needles oozed up my foot and calf.

It turned out that the young corporal was a cousin of the nervous man, and that both had been raised by their uncle, Ink-beard, after being sent away from the Shuravi-occupied zone as infants. It also turned out the cousins did not get along well. Not surprising, given that the younger cousin was a common soldier while the older did some kind of white-collar work that left his hands smooth and his nails perfectly trimmed.

The soldier seemed rather pleased to have brokered a meeting between his officer and his family.

On the third cup of tea, the elderly man asked what had prompted the officer and his guests to grace this house.

Finally! Time to get down to business. My American spirit sighed with relief. My Momand spirit cautioned it was too soon, though. I shifted my haunches to a less uncomfortable position on the hard floor and pretended to take another sip.

The officer looked at me and emptied his cup. It was refilled. He took a sip of his fourth cup and seemed to only then remember he'd been asked a question. "These two young men, sir. They claim to be of your wife's *tarbur*."

He'd married my cousin? Was she behind the screen? Which one? Nerie? Mariam? Bibi? Laila? Sharbat? I realized I was staring at the carved wood screen and jerked my gaze to a neutral spot. The teapot. Then I looked at the old man and bowed.

Clouded eyes under white brows moved from me to Oscar at my side and back to me. "Descendants of the Tiger?"

"I am Zarak, son of Abdul called Rund."

The nervous man went to the edge of the screen. After a whisper, he looked at me. "Please name the oldest sister of Mahmoud."

Which one was Mahmoud? And how should I know who was his sister? Unless they were my age, I didn't know any of the girls' names. Wait, there were two Mahmouds, at least. I couldn't address the person behind the screen, and the nervous man was too close to her. I met the old man's intent gaze and spoke to him. "I would ask if you mean the younger Mahmoud, called Bad Shoes, or the older Mahmoud whose brother tended my father's herd. In truth, however, I could name no sisters of either."

"Speak of she who watered the flowers."

My mind went blank. I had no idea who'd watered Grandmother's flowers.

Ink-beard studied me and made a gesture.

"Speak of the dragon."

Dragon? The paryan's terror? The one that killed Beowulf? Smaug? Then I remembered, and smiled.

The old man straightened up, looking affronted.

I dropped the smile. This was serious business. "In my mother's favorite poem, he lived by the sea. He danced in the autumn fog with the children of Honilee."

The old man lifted his cup and looked at me over the rim. "Speak of your father."

What would the tarbur have seen of my father? Very little, I supposed. He spent his time teaching, or reading to us boys, or rolling a ball for the little ones while talking with Mom. "He was an educated man, gentle and quiet. He taught history at the university in Kabul. When he came home from the city, he brought students, and they worked his fields. When those students moved on, more came from nearby. He had weak eyes, so he was called Rund. He was shot."

"Speak of his horse."

"His favorite was a tall gray stallion. When the stallion lost an eye, they said *Rund rides Rund.*"

He looked back at the screen. More whispering. The nervous man cleared his throat. "Are you the boy who read always?"

"No, that was my older brother, Hamid. He was called Talib. I was the roof climber, the Wezgórrey."

He cocked an ear to something I couldn't make out and nodded. "Speak of the little boy's eyes."

"My youngest brother's eyes are as unremarkable as my own. The boy just older than him would be Mohammed, whose eyes are the exact blue of our grandmother's special poppies."

"Why?"

The skin on my face tightened. *How dare you ask?* "Because God willed it so!"

Ink-beard blinked rapidly, and in the silence I realized my error. An honorable man does not snarl at an honorable woman, however indirectly. I bowed low over my shins, pressing my face into the faintly musty golden carpet. "Please forgive me, sir, for raising my voice in the presence of your family. I have no compensation to offer now, but if I live and if you give me your name, I will bring you the colt of a mare to give weight to my apology."

"Please, think nothing of this!" The old man glared over his shoulder toward the screen. "The question was not appropriate."

Calling it inappropriate implied a deliberate insult, but I'd bet he didn't mean to say so. His face paled rapidly, as if he'd just figured that out. He didn't volunteer his name.

The officer rose. "We have interrupted your day and importuned on your hospitality to an unforgivable degree. May you be safe and prosperous."

The old man touched his heart. "May your journey be safe and pleasant."

We were leaving. But we couldn't. Not when behind that screen was someone who knew where my people were. Who might know. Wait, wouldn't the old man or his wife have arranged the marriage?

I struggled to my feet, forcing a grace to my muscles, and was grimly amused to realize Oscar didn't have any weight on one of his feet. "Please, sir. Where has my khel moved?"

He looked at me from under those eyebrows. "Go to the center of town. At the well, face north. You will see in the distance a flag tower that appears to rise just to the left of the peak of the black mountain. Go west toward the barracks, crossing over the paved road, and you will find a goat track. Now when you look north, the flag should exactly line up with the peak of that mountain. This is how you know you have found the correct track. The track winds like a drunken goat but leads past the flag tower to a blue mosque where, inshallah, you may obtain further guidance."

Blue is the color of heaven, Grandson; it comes forth when the potter bakes salt into the tile.

My excitement tightened my throat, until I was sure it would choke me. I pictured myself fainting into Oscar's lap. That did it. I sucked in a long, deep breath. "How far, sir? A day? Two days?"

"Forty or forty-five kilometers, I believe, if you had a helicopter. Sixty, perhaps, as the track winds." He hesitated, plainly searching for words. "Hide yourselves along the way, especially as you sleep, for some of the people you will pass among are kafir. Others might be hungry enough to behave as kafir. Particularly, avoid the young. They are as savage as rats."

I touched my heart, thanking him. After all these years, street directions. Home was only two days' walk. The mental image of that flag tower pulled me, like an open bottle pulls a drunk.

Chapter Seventeen

Outside, the officer smoothly wished us a safe journey and said he was most happy to have given us a ride this far. Which meant we weren't getting arrested but also weren't getting a ride back to where our horses and saddles were. I'd be lucky to get our packs and weapons back out of that truck.

Oscar, standing on one foot and shaking the other, should have looked to some degree comical. Instead he looked like he was contemplating violence. But that was a great way to become a martyr, nothing more.

I thanked the officer for the ride and for carrying our packs and weapons—the burden of which we would relieve him now.

He said the long arms were very fine weapons indeed. Perhaps enough to cover the fine for crossing the border without documentation.

How courteous of him to establish the parameters of the bribe we'd need to get out of his sight. I could commence haggling by asking him if he was sure he was a Muslim, to demand so dear a price, but Pakhtunwali was older than Islam and demanded that I gift a man with anything he admired without restraint.

My little carbine was perhaps a fair price for being allowed to cross without repercussions, but sniper rifles like Oscar's were handmade, tailored to the individual, and if a man Oscar's age lost his rifle, he'd spend the rest of his military career parked at a desk. Oscar's weapon and career weren't mine to barter. So I agreed that they were very fine weapons, and in the same breath offered to purchase the long arms from him for the price of two fine young mares currently stabled at the communications hut west of here. The horses were worth rather less than our weapons would fetch in the right market, but might be sold much more quickly in any available market.

The officer slid his oily smile across his face and said he would sell us the carbine for the two mares.

If we could keep one weapon, it had to be Oscar's rifle. But I couldn't let on how valuable it was because then we wouldn't be able to afford it. Instead, I offered to let him keep some of the ammunition along with the mares.

He paused, peering into my eyes, clearly weighing my words and calculating how much he might profit or lose out of this. I didn't know how risk-averse he was, and that gave him an advantage. But he didn't know what to think of me, either.

At my back, Oscar bristled, but held his silence. I wasn't sure how much of this he caught, but somehow he had to play along, had to trust me.

I whispered, finally, that I would never forgive any man who stood between me and badal.

The officer moved closer, as if sniffing me, his garlicky breath hot on my mouth and chin.

An American would have moved back or pushed him back. I stared straight into the depth of his eyes. I could swear extravagant oaths, but I didn't know what would impress him and what would go too far.

Badal. Wasn't the one word enough? We were talking about the man who killed my baby brother Sorrow, who'd ridden my shoulder as I'd ridden our father's. My laughing little brother Ben, who'd wheedled money for that skateboard out of what I'd been saving for our trip home, who'd worked long hours in return for short riding lessons and then fallen asleep at the dinner table. Who'd become a man I didn't know. A man I would never know.

The officer snapped a sharp order.

The young corporal handed us the long arms, unloaded, and our packs.

If we were lucky, they'd dropped the ammo in the pack. I would probably have done the same if I planned to arm a man I'd stolen a horse from. If I was Pakhtun enough to have given back the arms.

The officer saluted smartly. "Your shells and knives are inside the packs."

"No doubt," I said politely and saluted back.

The truck left, stirring as much dust as an earthquake would before I had time to rewrap my shemagh.

I set out toward the cluster of rooftops that would be the town. "Once we have some distance and a degree of privacy, we can see what that smooth-talking pirate left us."

"Roger that." Oscar's tone was alarmingly clipped.

I cut my step to walk beside him. "How much of that did you follow?"

"Later. I don't like them knowing where to find us."

They had directions to my khel. Was Oscar saying he didn't plan to go there? "My home, my family, are two days' walk away. We can pick up horses, money, supplies—even a guide, maybe."

"'Sure, we'll help. Inshallah, bukhra.' Stopping there would get us nothing but spies and delays. The plan is to hurry to an ambush point—"

My ears burned. "To my family! Their help will make the difference of success or failure in this mission."

"Zulu, you haven't seen these people in close to twenty years. Trust me. They will disappoint you. Family always does."

I broke a sweat. "If I were a real Pakhtun, I would have to beat those words out of you."

He grasped my elbow, then let it go. "We'll get our bearings and find a road west. Unless I've misoriented us, a mujahid I used to know runs a smithy a village or two over. He'll get us on the right road."

"Are you certain he's still there and that you can find him right off the bat?"

"Nope."

"Then how is looking for your guy—who might not be there—an advantage over finding my people?"

He looked over his shoulder. "Our escort's turning around. Move."

He broke a run. I followed. We each took a wheel rut and ran, knees high and fists pumping, unsecured packs slapping against our backs. People looked at us, looked at one another, and edged out of the way. Shoppers and shopkeepers farther ahead looked at us and packed their wares hurriedly.

Children run all the time. When one man runs, people assume he's a thief or other fugitive. When two well-armed men run, without anyone crying thief or chasing them, there's a reason. So smart people get out of the way. If that means running, they run.

Questions echoed behind us: What is wrong? Where are they? I don't know. Why are we running? You stay and find out; I have children to raise!

We raced around a corner and through a bazaar proper, vaulting carts and baskets piled with dried dung, and soon landing in a flock of chickens. The chickens screeched and cackled and flew into the faces of old men. I coughed, inhaling down and dust. No good. I spit out a bit of feather and inhaled again through my shemagh.

Oscar slapped a goat, and on his cue I smacked another. The goats bleated and leaped. The rest of the herd exploded in random directions, two in a row landing on and bouncing off an overladen donkey who yelled *yee-haw, enough*! for once in his patiently miserable life and took to bucking. The donkey's pack broke loose, cheap aluminum pots clattering about his hooves and scattering as he kicked.

One kicked pot hit a goat from a different herd, who levitated vertically, turned forty-five degrees and tried to land on a stack of small TV sets. The TVs tumbled onto a yammering teenager in a turban, who balled up his fist and swung at me but missed. A choked bellow and cursing rose behind me.

A goat-abused cow bucked and contorted her bony self like a heifer, blasting out a hair-curling screech utterly unlike a *moo*. Small boys in candy-colored plastic shoes raced through, grabbing at the feet of squawking chickens and getting wing-beaten about the face and shoulders. One boy skidded in a fresh cow pie and fell, the chicken in his grip spewing feathers in every direction. I dodged him, careful not to land a boot on one of those thin brown limbs, but I didn't look back to see if he held on to the chicken.

We took another corner and Oscar dived into the ruins of a...oh no, a toilet. I took a heaving gasp of a breath and threw up into the hole in the bench. A chicken squawked and scuttled out of the way, then pranced back into view and looked hopefully up at me.

Oscar yanked his khaki shirt off over his head and whipped it inside out. The inside was black. He ripped the sleeves off, untucked the tail, and had a black vest over his green T-shirt, like half the men in the bazaar had worn.

I got control of my breathing, forcing myself not to smell, while watching him. I remembered my shemagh and wound it into a quick turban. My shirt wasn't reversible but I had my poncho liner to roll about my torso like the blankets so many men wore. I also yanked my cuffs out of my boots, shaking the sharper wrinkles out of the cloth. Civilians here didn't blouse their pant legs into their boots.

Oscar jammed his sleeves into his pack. I dropped the liner and my pack with it, rolled the pack and the M4 in the liner, and tied the bundle diagonally across my back over the sweatshirt. It wasn't anywhere near as ergonomic, but it worked.

I also noticed there weren't any magazines or shells in my pack. I was willing to bet Oscar had no ammunition either.

He stalked out into the sunlight and the billowing dust. After a moment I followed him. I wove left and right among knots of people babbling about the running men, and what was that all about. When someone asked me, I said God alone knew. And I kept walking.

We found a well-tended canal heading north and walked along the side of it. I wasn't going to challenge Oscar so long as we kept a heading toward the black mountain on the other side of the flag tower.

Where else did we have a chance of getting replacement ammunition, transportation, or even money? Where else but home?

Women stooping to fill brass pitchers or plastic jugs from the canal covered their faces as we passed, pausing in their work as if stillness could make them invisible. I looked away from them or over their heads. Whatever made them need to dip water from an open canal when there was a well in town, it didn't necessarily mean they were offering their forms or faces for any passing man's appraisal.

Heavy-limbed, gnarled trees grew on both sides of the canal. Sheep ambled among them as if looking for any scrap of green in reach. The larger, sturdier trees to the east had green leaf buds just beginning to show. The more delicate trees to the west were mostly dead gray, but a few had tiny flecks of pink. A pair of men in traditional *shalwar kamiz* were inspecting the budding ones, while two others were spraying the gray ones with a hand pump.

One of the inspectors spoke sharply. The men in the orchard turned to the southwest in unison, and each unfurled a mat or rug. Oscar whipped out his sleeves for us to kneel on.

I felt odd, going through the motions of prayer to avoid looking alien when so often I'd had to hide real prayer so I wouldn't be such an alien on the ship, in my chosen qawm. There was a lesson to be drawn; I struggled to put it in words. But with my hands cupping sunlight, I set aside that effort, clearing my mind to accept any truth offered in this moment of prayer.

Beside me, Oscar whispered, "He will gather us together and will in the end decide the matter between us in truth and justice..."

His words, the matter-of-fact way he said them, sifted into me. I could say the traditional prayer then, letting the wind take my whispered words as the sun warmed my face. The ancient words made me feel whole, comforted an ache I had not acknowledged in so long it had become a scar on my soul.

In the late evening, we stopped at a tiny mosque. A palsied old man was trying to light a lamp at the doorway, but between his shaking hands and the gusty wind, we saw him waste three matches.

"May you not be tired," I said when we reached conversational distance.

He overreacted, leaping back and sending the lamp sloshing on its hook.

I pretended not to notice. "Please, Uncle, may I demonstrate to my friend this new lighter I have?"

He swallowed, rolling his eyes. One solid-white eye pointed off to the side, but his other eye was dark, probably still worked. He brushed his hands down the front of his vest as if to brush away his flinch. "Of course, of course. Are you well and hearty?"

I nodded to the traditional greeting and ran a hand behind my back.

Oscar mashed the lighter into my palm and slid around me toward the lamp. The old man backed away warily, but Oscar just held up both of his big hands to shield the wick from the wind. Once I'd caught the light, he too backed away and bowed from the neck.

I gave the same bow to the old man. "Is there a hujra nearby, Uncle?"

"Of course. However, because of the foreigners and the army, they cannot invite you to stay there. When the army can break through any gate and carry away one's guests by force, who then dares offer hospitality?"

"Where then might strangers stay?"

He looked piercingly at me, then at Oscar. "I am an old man, but I prize what little life is left to me. If you understand I cannot protect you, nor even shut the gate between you and what brigands may lurk in the night, then you are welcome to stay here, in the courtyard or in the gallery."

I expressed my gratitude and followed him to the courtyard, where he bade us sit. He retired through a curtain and came back bent under a huge bundle of sheepskins.

"This at least I can offer. Take what comfort you may."

On his second trip, he brought a brazier and some charcoal to burn in it. The tea we were served was no more than hot water with mint and a touch of sugar, but a Pakhtun offers the best he has, so we drank it. The steaming cups did feel good. We blessed one another and one another's families.

I broke out packets of heat-and-eat kashi. It wasn't polite for guests to feed themselves, but in hard times, practicalities change the rules. At my insistence, the old man tasted it hesitantly, then encouraged me and Oscar to eat our fill. The old man offered a drizzle of ghee, which was old enough to taste like the yellow oil on movie popcorn, but it definitely improved the kashi.

I spilled a little ghee in my emptied teacup. If Oscar and I both lived long enough, I wanted something to anoint his brutally muscular ass with. Except that focusing on one another like that would shrink our chances of surviving. I regretfully set aside the thought. The ghee would be good with breakfast anyway.

After we'd chewed all we could, the old man produced a week-old newspaper. I embarrassed myself by how little of it I could read, but he praised my efforts and helped with the letters I didn't recognize. He assured me the problem was with the newspaper's choice of something-something, using words I didn't recognize that probably meant *font*.

If nothing else, this trip was improving my vocabulary.

Oscar sipped his hot water and watched us from the other side of the fire. He'd picked, of course, a vantage point that allowed him to watch both the inner doorway and the outer one without turning his head. From my seat rather nearer the fire, I could look up from the paper to see the dark archway that led to the street. I hoped any movement from the gallery would also catch the corner of my eyes.

Oscar's square face relaxed slowly. When the paper was folded, he stretched and yawned. I did too and helped the old man stand. He tottered away stiffly, leaving me and Oscar with the dusky red embers of the fire.

The old man might not allow himself to bar the door, but he hadn't said we couldn't. While I shoved a wedge under the outer street door, Oscar strung a line at shin height across the inner archway, attaching the line to something blocky, which I assumed was a noisemaker. I high-stepped over it, and we treated the interior doorways the same. Then we moved a few thick fleeces from the heap by the embers and spread them in a completely dark alcove near the gallery stair.

I realized Oscar was undressing. I slid a hand across his undershirt-clad back and over his shoulder and put my lips to his ear. "Do you really want to risk doing it tonight?"

He caught my hand with his callus-hard one. "I don't want to risk dying tomorrow, knowing I could have done it and didn't."

My heart beat harder, throbbing in my temples and in my belly. "Who gets bottom?"

He turned, still holding my hand against his shoulder. "I pay my debts."

That wasn't precisely the risk/benefit analysis I'd expected. I pulled back, but he held my hand. "If this is about squaring a debt, Oscar, never mind. I'm not twenty years old anymore. A night or two without isn't going to leave me all blue-balled."

"Don't talk with your mouth full of shit."

Which one of us is doing that? I didn't ask out loud, because he was enfolding my hand with both of his. I felt his pulse in my palm, my fingers.

"What's it like to undress with the same man again and again, to learn what he likes and how to tell when something's wrong?"

I sat on my ankles. "You don't know either, huh?"

He hesitated. "I don't like people knowing too much about me."

Those could have been my words. But I wanted to know about him.

In the darkness I slid my free hand down his chest, tugged his undershirt free of his waistband. I rested my hand on his knotted abdomen, listening and feeling as his breathing grew heavier.

My other hand came loose from his grip without resistance. I slid my hands around to his back, but that brought my face too intimately close to his face. I skimmed up the heated skin of his chest instead, his undershirt bunching against my wrists.

His aroma, rich and male, rolled over me. I buried my face in his undershirt, then pulled the cloth free and dropped it. Would it mean I knew him if I could pick him out blindfolded in a crowd?

His belt was unbuckled, his britches open. My hands slid down his flanks, under his waistline, and rested on the twin bulges of his warm, hard ass. "Is any part of you less than perfect?"

He grunted and grasped my sleeves. "Get all this off, because if I have to take it off, it won't be wearable tomorrow."

"Get the cup." My voice was as deep and rasping as his. *Testosterone. Yeah.*

I undressed while he fetched the cup, actually making noise that sounded as loud as an average mouse.

I smelled the ghee then. Ghee always smells warm. He pressed the cup into my hand. "Don't use it all, Zu."

My mouth went dry, but no. Another might never come for us, so I'd use as much as we needed. This needed to be right for him. I spread some on my cock, feeling for gritty particles and realizing I needed to wash in the ghee, since I hadn't washed in the tea. That's what clean bandannas are for, though. Wipe on, wipe off.

Wipe more on. More than three strokes and you're playing with yourself, they say. They're right. So I turned my attention to playing with Oscar. My oiled fingers opened his body, eased the way.

He pressed back against me. I took a cue from his methods and kept the fingering to a minimum. Some men like to chitchat before they dance, and some like their introduction at full tilt boogie.

Full tilt boogie introductions can seriously damage a first-timer. So despite his silent urging I rubbed the ghee in until it absorbed, then applied more. Lots more.

This, I figured, I could rub in with my cock. When I pulled his cheeks open and lined up, he stopped breathing.

"Exhale," I whispered. He did. When I felt his ribs expanding again, I pressed. He went rigid. I held position, waiting, knowing that getting the head in would be the worst of it. When he relaxed just that little bit, I pressed in more. The head popped in. Then he swallowed my shaft, as a hungry ass will.

That ring of tight muscle slid down my shaft and throbbed at the base. He was so hot inside, so much softer than anyone would believe from the hard-ass exterior. I held him, just a moment. Then before he could get to wondering about that, I withdrew.

The cold outside air made his ass even hotter now that that tight ring rested just below my head. I slid back in. Hot. Sweet. Pulled out. Relished the contrast of the cold air on my naked—

I didn't have a rubber on. "Fuck!"

"What?"

"Don't turn over and kill me. I just now figured out we're barebacking."

He inhaled slowly. "When's the last time you did that?"

"Never."

He laughed, the feeling like a hand clenching about my cock. "Carry on then."

What? But my dick was already in motion. I angled to rub across his prostate, and he bowed, gasping. *Want more of that? I'll give you more of that!*

If we'd had anything better than ghee to work with, I could have jackhammered his hole, and I bet he'd like it. But tonight I just pistoned inside him, rising on my knees more on one part of the stroke and lowering on another, giving the pump and thrust its own rhythm, and nudging that gland of his with every single thrust.

My balls swung between my thighs, accentuating every movement, brushing his warm skin every time my cock punched into his heated depths. This was the best part of being a man, feeling my balls swing and knowing what was in them. Feeling the swinging arc tighten as they drew close to my body for the shorter, harder strokes. Feeling the heat grow electric, almost painful. Knowing that I'd soon fly through paradise, even if I couldn't set foot and stay.

I belatedly remembered the reach-around. His hand was already there and knocked my hand away. I grasped his hips again, those powerful hips, and yanked them hard against me. My head prodded his gland, nuzzled it a bit more, then pulled back and thrust one last time.

Paradise! Rapid spurts jetted through me, the backblast of each igniting a pleasure so intense it burned me from the inside out. Oscar made a noise and convulsed. His ass pulled, squeezed, and wrung another set of spasms from my prostate.

    I fell forward across him, grabbing a mouthful of his short, thick hair and biting into it to keep from crying aloud.

Chapter Eighteen

The next day's walk was long. A bit before sunset, we drew near a larger walled enclosure. I looked up at the gun slits just below the top of the hujra tower, set at height-staggered intervals I'd seen before. My great-grandfather had decreed their placement, some high and some so low that every man and boy who could hold a rifle could help defend the khel.

I saw rifle barrels glinting now. Was I going to have to demand water? Had traditional Pakhtun hospitality deteriorated so much in one generation?

A window in the door cracked. A man coughed, shut it, coughed several more times behind it, and opened it. "May you not be tired."

I tried not to wilt with relief. From what I'd heard, that wasn't the open welcome it once had been. But it was something. "May you have peace, Uncle. I seek the hujra of he who is Hajji but before was called the Tiger."

The door swung open. "Enter quickly with your friend. The radio says there are foreigners about."

The men gathered in the hujra under a budding walnut tree hastily stood among the remnants of a skimpy-looking meal to shake hands. I recognized my grandfather, of course, and the old man sleeping gently by a sun-warmed wall was his father. My uncles had become gray-haired, hollow-cheeked, hawk-billed caricatures of themselves. My cousins were not the round-faced boys I remembered, but lean, hard men with what had been their father's faces. Some of those faces were bruised, and many of the hands were scraped and welted.

More tea was rapidly brewed, more naan brought out. I smelled almond sweets baking.

For an hour, we made agreeable, if sparse, conversation about the winter's end, the upcoming *Now Ras* festival, the condition of the flocks Oscar and I had observed on the way here, the way the Taliban meticulously counted each flock and took 10 percent.

Their choice of which ten, a man my age muttered, and the others shifted weight as to distance their opinions from his. With Oscar behind me, they should know I was no killjoy of a Talib, but a man with a family couldn't be too careful.

But no, they weren't looking at me. They instead threw sideways glances at my Uncle Abdallah. Who ignored them. Or pretended to.

Halwah and almond cakes were served warm with spicy ginger marmalade and more tea. Then rice came out, with a smallish pile of meaty curry. Oscar and I were urged to eat our fill, though only my grandfather shared the curry with us. The other men and boys ate rice, explaining apologetically they had filled their bellies before our arrival. More likely, there wasn't enough to go around. Turning a bleating animal into edible food takes more than the hour or so one could expect a guest to cheerfully wait.

My grandfather grunted that for all the years he had been granted to live, the students would be welcome to their 10 percent. He recalled for us the Shuravi, who had stolen a whole flock at a time—had indeed butchered any animal they didn't take and run trucks over the carcasses so that only dogs and evil birds might eat of them. The youngsters' eyes shone as they drank in stories of the retaliatory raids.

As mine doubtless had. Until the very end, I'd been too young to join in except to hold the horses in a safe place, out of sight. My legs had been too short to keep up as the men flowed from nook to cranny among the rocks toward the final target, my little-boy arms not strong enough or long enough to properly wield one of the precious rifles.

By American standards, I'd been a little boy. Here, just too small and too inexperienced a warrior for such raids. Until that last one, the disaster.

One of the uncles explained to the youngsters that *Shuravi* had meant *friend*, until it had come to be used for the Soviets. I wasn't sure about that, but the matter wasn't mine to dispute.

Another cousin mentioned the neighbor's fond hopes the government would come fix the bridge on the highway so they could stop paying a cup of barley for every head of livestock driven over the bridge my uncles and cousins had built.

I sipped a few drops of green tea from my cup. I didn't want to be the first one here to fill my bladder. I had to watch where someone else emptied it before I hit that level of need.

The seeds I had brought were a paltry gift compared to the gifts I would need to accomplish my badal. Before I asked anything of these, my people, I had to establish bonds of a man with men, not of the shadow of a little boy who would, on a dare, climb anything that jutted toward the sky.

One boy, maybe twelve or thirteen, held his mouth gracelessly open, displaying canines that had grown in crooked, just like my brother Omar's, and just like an uncle whose name I couldn't remember. He breathed harshly too, making me want to take a look at his adenoids. But not tonight.

I took another six or eight molecules of tea and praised its scent. Now was the time I should tell them of myself and my family. My mouth opened—and closed with nothing said.

I looked again at the bruised faces and the scraped, bruised hands and forearms. Either they'd been in a riot, or they'd recently played buzkashi. A few of my uncles had an unbounded passion for the sport. "So, who among you threw the boz into the circle of justice?"

The openmouthed cousin sat up straight, his eyes glittering in the firelight. It had been a hard-fought game. The kind of epic game that starts one morning, restarts the following dawn, and ends just before evening prayer. Three of the boys elbowed one another and spilled bits of stories, fragments not yet patchworked together for the version that would enthrall generation after generation here in the hujra, as boys warmed their hands by the burning droppings of the many-times-removed grandkids of the goats whose droppings warmed us now.

And maybe that's what home was. Speaking before their elders was forward of them, a fact their fathers would no doubt let them know about later. But for now they were vastly entertaining and were fondly tolerated.

My great-grandfather yawned and stretched. Two of the cousins hurried over, handed him his teeth, and half carried him to the stool beside me, which an uncle hastily vacated. I stood, touched my heart, and shook his fragile, ancient hand. Oscar did the same.

The hajji was given a cup with maybe an ounce of tea trembling in the bottom of it. Any more, and he would have spilled it.

The conversation took up again. Someone mentioned my cousin Bad Shoes. I tensed, abruptly remembering his sneer. *Your mother left her father's home to find a husband.*

I sipped another half drop of tea, willing the cup to hold still in my hand.

Bad Shoes had taught me a lot about fighting. When I'd gone to America, I'd used those lessons, busting noses and lips with wild abandon in my first schoolyard fight, taking out all my frustration and anger—and, yes, fear—on two other fourth-graders. They'd finally cowered against the fence, crying like little children, while I taunted them to stand up as if they had balls. When big hands grabbed me, I spun, fist cocked, and stopped dead. The old woman held me, the aide. I couldn't hit a woman.

And putting such fear in an old woman's eyes was shameful to any Pakhtun with a mother.

I dropped my fist and bowed, apologizing sincerely for having frightened her. Which is probably why, instead of being expelled, I got my first round of anger-management counseling and a full-time cultural transition aide.

But I'd missed something in the conversation around me. I focused. Bad Shoes had sponsored the game, with attendant feasts for all comers, to celebrate the circumcision of his third son. The cost should have beggared him, yet he still had six fine horses and his sons attended school. No one actually said anything might be amiss, of course. It was all in the shift of eye and shoulder, the trailed-off sentences.

I emptied my cup. My great-grandfather refilled it for me, splashing only a little on my wrist and knee. The scald was slight, and I saw it coming just far enough to dampen any reaction.

But then I froze. His cup was still full enough to slosh way up the sides with his hand's palsy. Was I supposed to refill it anyway, or offer to?

Doing nothing was an action, probably the wrong one, so I bowed to him over the fire. "My *Baba* surely taught me whether to refill the Hajji's cup, but after all these years, the memory becomes elusive. Please, advise a traveler correctly."

He smiled kindly. "My cup is far from empty. Family is the root of all good things God the Compassionate has put on this earth, is it not?"

"As the wise have said, so surely it must be. In the darkness of strange places, I often comforted myself and my brothers with the stories of our forefathers."

"Who are your brothers?" The crooked-toothed boy. Had he been so forward with only his uncles and forefathers present, he would've been promptly backhanded. But he'd asked what no man could be coarse enough to directly ask, and their relief was palpable.

I took a gulp of tea. The air went still. "My brothers were Hamid, Omar, Mohammed, and Sorrow."

"*Wezgórrey!*" A thin, heavy-bearded man tackled me, laughing in delight, knocking my head into Oscar's lap and kissing me right and left and right again, his beard scouring my wind-chapped lips. "It truly *is* you! You came home!"

I grasped his upper arms, felt the knob of an old break below his right shoulder. Recognition tightened my grip. "Kam Ali! You know me still?"

Amid shouts of *Mashallah!* he held me tight against him and suffered my hug in return. "We knew you would return, inshallah, wherever your destiny took you. From heart to heart, there are ways."

Another whooping cousin yanked me from his arms. I laughed helplessly, embarrassed as any American man, but let them sling me from one embrace to the next. Someone handed my great-grandfather a Kalashnikov; he emptied a deafening burst into the tree branches overhead, raining twigs and sticky green buds among us.

I caught a glimpse of Ali, still laughing wildly, jerking Oscar's face east and west for enthusiastic kisses.

The chant of thanksgiving rose with a shower of sparks. *"For he who was lost is found! He who was dead is returned to us! Mashallah, Wezgórrey is home! Mashallah!"*

Clapping started, and a handful of my cousins danced to the beat. My uncles joined, and the rest of the cousins. I held back, until my grandfather insistently waved me to join, and waved Oscar to join me.

We danced until I was breathless. Afterward, my uncles told me a "Ben" had come to them with a horse any man might kill for. He'd told stories of the family, and asked if they knew the family he sought. They'd been hospitable—of course, of course!—but Rund had no son named Ben, and the man had sounded oddly like a Nangrahari, like me. And his companion had smiled too much.

Ben's riding companion had come back alone days later, and had finally left without the bedraga to Pekhawar he'd demanded. No one of the khel knew or liked him well enough to grant him safe escort. Yes, he had returned with Ben's rifle. No, he did not return with Ben's beautiful mare.

But Bad Shoes had left an hour after him and had taken the family's only running truck and cargo trailer.

I showed them the printouts. They turned up the lamps and a crank-powered lantern. Yes, this was the Ben who had come to them, and yes, this was his companion. Alas that they had denied him! And yes, they would certainly finance badal against he who had murdered a son of Rund.

They studied Oscar's face and withheld comment but pressed halwah and candied fruit into his hand.

They pieced together two cracked, scribbled-upon, stained, torn maps and argued over which roads to Pekhawar, other than the well-patrolled highway, were truckworthy. Then they traced out the horse trails that cut far more than half the distance of the truck's best routes. I explained the map to Oscar.

His eyes glittered in the flickering light. A little after that, when consensus had been reached but not everyone had tired of chewing the possibilities, Oscar pointedly yawned. I took the hint and said we must leave early to intercept the kafir traitor.

My grandfather stood, as did the uncles and older cousins. I realized they were going inside, to bed, and remembered the seeds. "Wait, please, Grandfather. I have a gift for the mothers." I thought of round seeds getting dropped on the ground and trampled. "Could someone please bring some flat dishes or school slates with raised rims?"

They brought slates like I'd learned to write and do my math on. The men jostled about me, exclaiming as I poured the seeds from each twist of paper onto a schoolboy's slate and carefully caught any round one that tried to roll toward the edge. The sunflowers were admired. The okra, lentils, and beans were received with respect but not admired. The three packets that might be tomatoes or peppers were discussed with animation. I took it the crops hadn't been good in the last few years. The tiny black seeds were fingered and speculated over. Perhaps they were something-something, perhaps something else—the words were ones that brought no memory or image to my mind. Kam Ali cried aloud over the two groups of watermelon seeds and a dozen seeds that might be cucumber but inshallah might be cantaloupe. All their melons had been lost in two consecutive unlucky years, and none of their wives or children had tasted such luxuries since then.

Amid the pushing and exclamations, it occurred that I should have brought much larger quantities to avoid strife over the division of scarce supplies. How many hills could a dozen seeds plant, after all? Then, with relief, I remembered that this was specifically not my problem. My duty ended when I gave the seeds to my grandmother, the senior mother. She or whoever she designated would divide them as the women saw fit, according to rules no man had a right to ask about.

The seeds were rewrapped with a gratifying reverence and were taken inside. I wasn't invited to take them, but maybe that was because Oscar couldn't be allowed indoors. Seeing my grandmother again, after all these years, would have been nice. But asking to see her or asking why I couldn't would be insufferably rude.

Maybe there would be other visits, other chances.

Oscar and I were given a large string bed with thick, clean fleeces to go under us and blankets to go over. Shivering from our bath, we climbed in with Kam Ali—whose wife was pregnant yet again—snuggled between us.

I slept fitfully, waking here and there to hear Kam Ali talking about one of my childhood escapades.

Or Hamid's. I was pretty sure the toad in Grandfather's bed was Hamid's trick.

I wondered a few times, irritably, why Oscar would want to lose sleep listening to such crap. Eventually, though, I realized Oscar was asleep. I tickled my cousin's eyelash, but it didn't so much as flutter. He'd been sleep-talking.

I smiled. No wonder his wife wanted him out here, sleeping in the hujra with the unmarried men. I rolled him over to point his voice toward the tree trunk and so I could take the middle spot, and slept wedged between his back and Oscar's.

Chapter Nineteen

Kam Ali and his oldest son, age twelve, went with us. So did my Uncle Abdallah, who told me he owed his right leg, if not his life, to my father's willingness to risk his own life and two fine horses carrying him to the big hospital in Jalalabad.

Abdallah brought his nephew Short Omar, whose father and older brothers had all been killed with Hamid. Short Omar plainly had Down syndrome. Oscar gave several hard looks, passing from Omar to me, as we packed our saddlebags in the lamplight. I shrugged. If he couldn't function, no one would have proposed including him.

We left well before dawn, leaving behind Oscar's prized rifle because without ammo it was an expensive and not particularly ergonomic club. We carried locally made Kalashnikovs instead and a hundred rounds each. We wore the local shalwar kamiz civilian uniform.

We rode hard in the moonlight, recklessly. Given the condition of the truck they'd taken, the diminished size of its often-repaired petrol tank, the condition of the roads, and the location of supplies along the way, my uncle was sure he could plot Tango's route and his schedule for arriving at each point along the way. He said there would be one last chance to catch the man. I believed him.

The sun rose. We stopped at a hujra where Abdallah was known and traded out horses with no more than ten words of conversation. Badal is a potent word. Nobody wanted to delay a lascar for blood vengeance. They'd hear the story later, inshallah.

We traded horses again at noon and again an hour later. Lunch was the same as breakfast, jerky and gobs of mutton tallow chewed in the saddle. That fourth set of horses had to last us until late afternoon when we finally stopped to eat and rest, alhamdulillah.

Trying to dismount, I fell out of the saddle. Oscar caught me. "Ass numb?"

"Totally. And I am not the least bit sarcastic." I grinned wryly at Abdallah and Ali, who looked concerned. "I have not ridden so before. You might have to beat me with a thorn branch to keep me moving at this pace."

"Badal," Kam Ali reminded me, his tone worried.

I nodded. "Nothing else matters until it is khallas."

At dusk, we reached a highway. There Abdallah whipped out three cell phones and checked one. "Three bars. This is enough."

He passed me a cell phone and passed Kam Ali another. "We two will hide here and call if they come. Kam Ali, cut across. Find a lookout over the intersection by the hawk's shadow's shrine. Zarak, you must ride two kilometers north on this road, to where it merges with two others. If I call you to say he is on the high road, he will come there. If Ali calls you to say he is on the low road, hurry along the northernmost track to the bomb crater deep enough to swallow two horses, and then cut due east to a bridge by a shrine. He must come by there."

I checked my phone, which unsurprisingly had three bars as well. "What's your number?"

He pointed to the speed dial interface. "I have number one. Ali has number two. You have number three. Hurry to find a good place before full dark. Sleep well. They will probably come soon after dawn."

I caught another hard look from Oscar. *Yes, Oscar. The fact he's snapping out orders instead of spending two hours building a consensus probably does mean my Uncle Abdallah has military training, which probably does mean he's hard-core Taliban. But for this mission he's my uncle. Ben's uncle. We ride for badal.*

Oscar found a shelf cave and used his vest to sweep debris and unfriendly crawlers out of the wind-sheltered part. We didn't build a fire, just got naked together with sheepskins piled over and under us and the horses tethered between us and the mountainside. The moon rose slowly.

Oscar wrapped an arm around my waist and pulled me closer, nudging me with his hard cock. "I have some tallow. Body heat should turn it into the slickest stuff you'd want. Unless you'd rather concentrate on the job at hand."

That self-containment was not Pakhtun. We had, centuries ago, named ourselves Afghani, which roughly translates as the Rowdy Bunch. That name didn't suit either me or Oscar. Yet—Afghan or not—he had led me back to my Pakhtun core, and I had found its echo in him.

We are the Desert People, he'd said. *Warriors.* And, for the night, this warrior was mine.

I leaned briefly against him, then looked out over the shelf of rock, over the road below. Far in the distance, possibly on the other side of the river, I saw a tiny fire. If we could see through stone, we would be able to look in the opposite direction through our mountain to the broad Swat Valley, where there were too many roads, too many people, and too few mountainsides from which to spring an ambush. Tango could go to Pekhawar or past it to the military base at Abbottabad. Or he could stop short at too many potential places to even guess at. Too many options. "We have to stop him here."

"Inshallah."

We laughed together. It wasn't funny. It was just good to have someone understand me. "I'd love to use that tallow on you, Oscar, but I'm so tired I don't even know if I could get it up."

He nuzzled my ear. "All you have to do is spread out and let me play."

I thought of wrestling him for it. But he'd win. Unless, of course, I injured him. But what fun would that be? Though the thought of wrestling had sure warmed up my crotch. My dick wasn't exactly standing up, but it wasn't just lying there either.

He rolled something between his hands. "Be glad I've been softening it."

I pried apart his hands and the lanolin smell of mutton tallow hit me. "Do you know how long that smell will stay in your skin?"

"I'll deal with it." He brushed his chin, still not whiskery, against my bristle. "Roll over."

"You ever do it face to face?"

"Why would I want to do that?"

Well, if we had light, so I could see your face as you came. I shook my head. We didn't have a lot of moonlight, and moonlight isn't a whole lot by itself.

He kissed my shoulder. I flinched. He held me. "Zu?"

"I'm not used to being kissed."

"You got an objection to it?"

No. It was just strange. I shook my head.

He kissed my neck, gently but with lots of tongue, biting the edges of my beard. "I love the way you smell."

He was crazy. I'd been riding all day since my last bath, and I hadn't worn deodorant since a couple of baths ago.

He kissed the base of my throat, then used his head to push me over on my back and kissed the base of my sternum. I knotted my hand in his hair. "Wait."

"What?"

"You don't have to blow me to get me to spread my cheeks for you."

"Good." He turned his head and kissed my cock, which bounced against his cheek. "Because I'm not sure I'll be any good at this, and I'd hate for my chances to ride on it."

I'd never heard of a bad blowjob except in a joke. Oscar's wasn't a joke. He was surprisingly gentle, and careful with his teeth. It took a long time, given how tired I was, but he was patient. And, by the time I came, the tallow bar in my ass had melted to liquid.

I rolled over sluggishly, inviting him with a spread.

"I hope you don't expect this to last long," he muttered.

I didn't expect anything. I was still floating warmly, free of thought or calculation of any sort.

He prodded, prodded harder, stretching me right out of my warm floatiness, and slid in with a burn-inducing abruptness.

It seemed to surprise him too. "Whoa!"

"Whoa," I whispered into the fleece.

"What?"

"Go, man. Go."

He did, short-stroking as if the blowjob had tuned his nerves and gotten him halfway there, more like fucking than foreplay. In just a few moments he went rigid, then convulsed against me. "Bravo!"

I lay there, blinking in the dark, my brother's name echoing off the rocks in my head. No wonder he didn't want to do it face-to-face. Not where he might catch any glimpse of my hawk face instead of Ben's smooth, handsome features.

It served me right. Thinking like a romantic. Not like a warrior.

I turned over, shoving him off me, and climbed to another rock. I knelt for a moment and then stood. Just me and the biting wind and the ice-crystal stars. I let the wind blow through me, scour me out, make me a warrior. Only a warrior.

"Zu?"

I looked down at him, his worried face. Did he even know what he'd said?

It didn't matter. I would use his warmth to get through the night well rested. I would use his strength and his warrior's prowess tomorrow. Badal. Only badal.

And if I didn't have to worry about hiding Oscar's face from Tango, I'd wipe my ass with his shemagh.

* * *

I stood before the TV and watched, mashallah, as the Shuravi left my home. I wept with the mujahidin on the screen and with them cried aloud my gratitude. Mashallah, mashallah!

Then I turned to practicalities. "Now we can go home."

"Use your English, Ricky," my mother's father chided, holding his finger in place on his magazine page. He looked expectantly over the rims of his glasses.

"My name is Zarak!"

Omar clutched his new Game Boy against his chest and looked from one of us to the other. "What is wrong?"

"English!"

I took a deep breath, trying to think of English words for planting barley, moving flocks to summer pasture. After the massacre, my khel would need every man's hand. In the end, I could only shrug and use the child's English I knew. "It's time to go home."

"You *are* home, Ricky. Get used to it."

I turned back to the television. "My name is Zarak."

Omar tugged my sleeve. "We must obey him, Ricky."

I punched him hard. "He is a kafir! We must go *home.*"

My mother's father stood, roaring. "*Time out!* Time out for you, you little punk! See if I let you watch any more TV for a *week!*"

Showing respect to my mother's father took a struggle in the best of times. He smoked tobacco without shame, and ate pork without being driven by hunger to the unclean meat. He drank wine with dinner once or twice a week. He played piano in mixed company. He *taught* piano, to male and female alike. And he had allowed his oldest daughter to leave his home to seek her own husband.

But the point remained that I would need airplane tickets to get us all home. So I dedicated myself to earning the money for those tickets.

Chapter Twenty

The cell phone woke me up. Abdallah's voice. "Bismillah, he comes! Expect him in three or four minutes. Our truck is being pulled by another truck."

"Do both trucks have the same size tires? If we could take out a tire on the other truck, so he must ride horseback or walk, he'd be naked to the wind."

"I didn't look at that, and now they are out of sight. The trucks are much the same size, though."

I dressed hurriedly, leaning on a rock because one leg was asleep "How accurate are you with an AK-47, Oscar? Can you take out a slow-moving truck's tire with it?"

"Bet your ass."

I looked at him. His smile faded. His brows rose, then smoothed into the blank masklike face I wanted.

But that moment's expression answered my question. He didn't have any idea what he'd said last night.

Oscar and I crouched in the middle of the road, our borrowed Kalashnikovs on our backs. The weapons, more than our borrowed local clothing, said we weren't American, weren't NATO. The flat, greasy smell of mutton fat hung in a cloud about us. Or at least about me. I couldn't escape it. No more than I could escape Oscar, or the memory of his voice calling my brother's name.

The truck wheezed around a curve, slowly in case a new crater had opened on the other side, and saw us. The truck downshifted, slowed, and blasted its horn. Oscar had his back to it. "Is he in the front?"

I stood, gingerly because my leg was asleep, and stared through the windshield. Oscar, still below hood level so they'd have a chance of tipping the truck if they just ran over him, buried his knife between the front right tire's tread and, just as quickly, yanked it loose.

The Chihuahua came out yapping. He was taller than me. Most Americans are. He outweighed me by a little, not a lot. But he yapped like a dog.

He'd left my brother for the dogs.

I smiled. "Hello, there."

He kept yapping, mixing Dari with Pashto and Arabic and some shit I didn't recognize, swearing he was on a holy mission and my soul would drink burning water forever if I held him back.

I lunged at him, but the numb leg folded under me. With a desperate prayer, I put my weight on the leg I could feel.

The dog turned and leaped back into the truck.

Before he completely shut the door, I caught it and braced against his frantic pull. Smiling, I climbed onto the step and leaned into his face. "I don't believe we have been introduced."

"God protect me!" The driver moaned. "Feranghi and more feranghi! Why did I stop? Why?"

"Because you saw the promise of money?" I suggested in the same language, but my eyes didn't leave Tango. He was so close I couldn't focus my vision, but I didn't have to. He wouldn't be able to focus either, and that might keep him off balance while I clenched and released the muscles in my numb leg, willing it to wake up.

"You spoke English," he said.

"Yep."

"You can't arrest me. You have no authority here. We're in Pakistan. You'd have to go through extradition and all kinds of shit."

"Please, do not kill him in my truck! Please! I have a family!"

"We are in the land of the Pakhtun. Something you should—" In midsentence, I closed my hand on Tango's throat and turned, bracing against the dashboard and the seat to thrust him out of the cab and onto the ground below.

He hit his feet like a gymnast and turned toward the back of the truck.

I hobbled after him, the nerves in my leg burning to life. He couldn't escape. Not now. But my leg folded at the knee. I couldn't catch him. "*Oscar!*"

A chuckle came on the wind. "Let him come, Zarak."

The dog stopped. Spun to face me.

"No..."

I jumped him, slamming him back against the packed dirt road. His breath gusted out, but he still swung at me.

I punched under his swing, burying my fist in his solar plexus.

He jackknifed, his face purple. I considered a few kicks to keep him down, but I didn't want to explain to Pakistani police why I'd kicked a man to death in the middle of the road.

Instead I dropped a loop of Oscar's 550 parachute cord over each of his fists, flipped the long ends of the cord over his head so they encircled him. Then I planted a knee in his chest and snatched the cord tight, yanking his arms into a parody of a self-hug. I knotted the cords tightly before he could catch his breath or figure out what was happening.

A man fights having his hands drawn behind him. It's an awful lot easier to secure them in front, then resecure them in the rear under more controlled conditions, alhamdillulah.

The driver was praying loudly. I heard hoofbeats and a whinny from the trailer behind the towed truck. I stepped back and unslung my Kalashnikov, in case it wasn't Ali or Abdallah. But it was Abdallah.

I stood back and let him take control. He assured the driver we would not interfere in his escape and in the name of justice offered him a lakh toward a new tire.

The driver recovered his balls and commenced bellowing insults and demands. Two Kalashnikovs clacked, going off safety. The driver shut up.

Oscar squirmed under the towed truck and out again as rapidly. "Khallas. Broken axle."

I translated.

Abdallah's face dropped. "As God wills, it is meant to be."

Ali arrived with his son, and the two of them slung Tango belly-down over his son's skinny gelding. Ali took the gelding's reins while his son—face aglow—took possession of Tango's mare and all of the tack in the trailer. I collected Oscar's horse and mine, and we rode away before any of the morning traffic happened upon us.

On a side trail, we reined in and offered to gag Tango. I didn't see how he had the wind to yell and swear like that, with a wooden saddle smacking him repeatedly in the chest and belly. He told Oscar he was an American citizen and had rights.

I stroked my beard. "This is true, but you have rejected the US, have you not?"

He twisted to look at me, though his shemagh sagged over his eyes. "Who are you?"

"You know who I am." I adjusted my sunglasses and did a few stretches. They felt good, but then I hadn't spent much time at all in the saddle yet today. How long would it take to truly get used to riding like this?

More time than I could possibly take.

"No," he said earnestly. "I don't. But you're American, right?"

I thought about it for a moment, but Oscar wouldn't have used my name back there on the road if it wasn't expected to mean something to him. So this was an attempt at manipulation. I didn't feel like playing his games. "You're lying."

"I need sanctuary. Nanawatai. You have to give it to me if I ask, right?"

"Wrong."

Kam Ali rode close and dropped his hand on my shoulder. "Kill him, son of my uncle. Then you can send your man home with his ears and you can stay with us. We will ride as brothers, always."

I wanted to. We'd ridden, more as brothers than as cousins, a long time ago. But that was a long time ago.

If diplomatic conditions normalized, I could finish my twenty years and retire here. My savings and my pension would go a long way in the local economy, wouldn't they? But if I stayed now, I'd be called a deserter. At best, I'd be a burden on the family. The family didn't look like it could take a lot of burdening.

"I don't understand you," Oscar said politely. He'd been riding drag, and his shemagh was stiff with dust.

The dog yapped again, wheedling. "Oscar, you can't let foreign nationals take me. I deserve protection."

"Shut up, Tango. Luckily for you, what you deserve has nothing to do with it."

Something occurred to me. "Oscar, what was that about the major's boys taking the blame if we didn't bring this one back for trial?"

He looked at the sky while his mount fidgeted. "I don't know the details, but someone dispatched an army patrol to the murder scene. Given the timing, it doesn't look like they would have been able to save him, but they could have limited the"—he looked away—"the collateral damage. Saved more evidence. But a man riding a beautiful Arabian mare and leading another horse intercepted them near the road and assured them they didn't need to investigate, that this was an OGA matter."

A patrol would have had to hike quite a ways, from the nearest truck-safe road. They'd taken the easy answer. In Afghanistan, the easy answers are almost always the wrong ones.

I still didn't see how having Tango presented for court-martial would save anyone's ass. But maybe not bringing him, after coming so far to get him, would cost Oscar, or Mike. My personal feelings aside, they'd acted to secure justice for a brother marine, exactly as Pakhtuns would have.

I looked at Uncle Abdallah. "Is this telephone such a one that would allow me to call the USA?"

"What telephone?" He asked blandly. "Do you think it will rain today, Wezgórrey?"

"Somewhere on earth, Uncle, surely." I handed the phone to Oscar. "Tell me you can call the cavalry."

He looked at me a moment, his face still entirely hidden by sunglasses and shemagh, then walked around the skinny gelding and looked down at Tango.

Tango twisted to stare at him, then at me. "In God's name, *baradur*..."

"You're not my brother," I said coldly.

* * *

Twenty-two hours later, a USMC Huey UH-1 Y "Yankee" helicopter, one of the smallest they make, hovered a foot above the ground a mile north of my grandfather's khel. Tango refused to board, so Oscar and I bodily slung him in. Then we climbed in.

Inside, he and I sat at the open bay door, trying to ignore Tango. Oscar pitched his voice under the roar of the motors, the rotors, and the wind. "What did I do?"

I looked out at the morning sky. "You completed your mission. Or close to it."

"So why are you pissed?"

I studied my dusty boot toes. "My name isn't Bravo."

He recoiled.

"*Allahu!*"

I looked up.

"*Akbarrrr!*" Tango tackled me like a fullback, driving me out through the open bay. We fell.

I clawed and kicked in the rushing icy air. My fingertips brushed Tango's sleeve. I caught his wrist, locked my fingers about it. A shocking jerk jolted up my arm, and I stopped falling. We both stopped, though the wind tore at our clothes.

I dangled one-armed from the end of his arm. He thrashed, but I held on, eyes closed against the blasting wind, waiting for my weight to tire him. He stopped thrashing. I squinted against the wind and saw a dark sleeve coming at me, with a leading edge of glittering steel.

My own choora found my free hand and arced up to meet his. Blocking that first wild slash sent a thrill through me, gave me strength and speed to slash back. The long tip of my blade caught in his sleeve.

I had to yank it free. I needed to concentrate on jabbing, not slashing. Jabs would be harder to block.

Tango seemed to be hanging from the dark mouth of the helo by his knees, but from his renewed struggles—even with my weight dangling from the end of his arm—he'd like nothing better than to plunge headfirst into the afterlife.

If anything held him to the helo, it would be Oscar. If anyone could hold him, my lifeline, Oscar could.

His blade came at me again, edge-first at my gripping arm. I thrashed, turning my body so his blade slashed along the back of the arm. Blood spilled into the wind—a lot of it. He must have cut to the bone. That would hurt, inshallah, bad and soon. If it didn't, I'd be dead.

Losing my extensor tendons there wouldn't keep me from holding on. I had to protect the vulnerable inner surface of my arm; if he damaged the tendons that clenched my fist, I would fall.

I had to do a chin-up to reach him, stabbing for the axial nerve plexus in his armpit. He elbowed my blade aside, so I cut his arm where I could reach it. More blood gushed into the torrential wind.

I couldn't tell what was noise, what was cold, what was wind. They all beat at me.

I parried his next swing, and another, then pulled up again to jab for something that would count. The wind swung us both, or my gyrations did, or his did.

Blood poured up my arms, hot at the cut but cold as it coated my elbows. If I shifted a single finger from wrist or from knife hilt, the slick blood would keep me from ever gripping again.

He screamed profanities worded as prayer. He wanted to die. Wanted to take me with him, as an apostate to serve him forever after this life.

If I died today, inshallah, it would be with true prayer in my mouth. "La ilaha ilallah!"

He slashed at me again and opened a nick just below the elbow of my gripping arm. Blood spit a red trail in the wind.

I aimed, did my pull-up, and opened the brachial artery in his chest. In exactly the hollow where I would have rested my head, had I died in Oscar's arms.

Tango cut at me again, desperately, and I slashed open his inner arms, one and then the other, sending his knife flying into the ice-laden wind. Blood spurted.

I didn't blink fast enough. It blinded me.

I hung on. Tango's struggles weakened and stopped. The wind pounded at me, flapping my loosening shemagh against my face and ears until the cloth whipped away, fluttering, like a kite without a string.

Oscar was shouting. I couldn't hear. Noise. Cold. Noise. Wind. Grit stinging my face and arms.

Grit? Sand...ground?

I opened my eyes and through the blood smear saw sand, pebbles, a straggly line of za'atar bushes scratching at my ankles. I let go and fell. The ground hit me, knocked the wind from me. But that wasn't the problem. I was…cold. Tired. Sleepy.

Something heavy and limp landed beside me. Then Oscar jumped and crouched over me, blocking out the sky. The sky darkened behind him.

"Don't fade, Zu. Hang on."

He pried open my eyes and poured icy water under my lids. Then hunched over me as the wind rose, beating at me and trying to freeze my scarf to my face and jaw. My arm hurt. He was pouring a powder into the wound there. A soothing heat built up, and the blood went from spurt to ooze.

Some part of my educated mind whispered the name of the clotting agent, the rules for using it and how…how to…

"Zulu! Stay with me!"

I remembered my brother's body, my cousins' bodies, my uncles' bodies, all lined up and most of them identified. My grandfather guided my hands, showed me how to wash what was left of Hamid's torn body, the right side and then the left, how to bind his ankles and turn his face toward Mecca. I wept, and my grandfather's tears fell hot as blood on my neck, but his voice never wavered as he told me death was but the second birth, less painful for most, and necessary to open the way to true life.

"Momand!" Oscar slapped me. "Zarak Momand!"

"I fucked the vein, Gunny. This ain't working."

"Make it work," Oscar growled.

"Well, fuck. Where else can I try?"

"How the fuck should I know? Get on the phone and ask! Zarak!" Something stank, burned up my nose, unbearable. I turned away. The burning smell followed me.

Out of sight, other men talked. Trauma room discussion. *Jugular vein. Behind the ear down to the collarbone here. Take a second to study the diagram. Stick your finger here, right above the collarbone. Slide the needle into the vein at a real low angle...*

Something stung my neck. I tried to move, tried to swat the bug, but Oscar's knees held my head, and Oscar's hands held mine.

Something real cold went through the side of my head, seeped through my brain. I shivered helplessly.

"Wezgórrey! Ricky!"

I tried to shake my head, but something held it still. "My name is Zarak."

"Then sit *up*, Zarak."

I sat up, to my astonishment, and almost passed out. Oscar caught me about the shoulders.

A pale young man stood over me, holding a plasma bag, the clear liquid catching the sunlight and reflecting it piercingly into my eyes.

I took a couple of deep breaths, scented with the faintly Listerine-like flavor of za'atar and ammonia somewhere. I felt...better.

I tried to find a nonbloody part of my sleeve to wipe my eyes, then saw a stack of bandages and used the top one of those.

The youngster's shadow swayed.

I looked up and saw the taut face, the white line around his mouth. My protective instinct stirred. "You. Sit down. Now."

He sat, hard, and looked surprised. "Yes, sir... Doc."

He was a one-striper, probably eighteen or barely nineteen. Poor kid. At least he held the plasma high overhead, so it would keep dripping its restorative magic into my neck. The helo passed over us again, and we all shivered in the blasting wash of wind. "Can't that thing land?"

"No, Doc. Not anywhere nearby. We're going to have to bring you up in a body basket. You and...uh...it."

I looked in the direction he couldn't. Tango's sleeves had caught in the branches of a shrub or young tree, and his blood leeched into the sandy ground amid the broken herbs, drawing a line toward another taller bush. I realized the herbs were lines between young trees, and that Tango's body had broken half the branches off one. Well, what lived would be heartily nourished; the gardener wouldn't lose all that much, inshallah.

This clotting stuff needed to get out of my arm before lack of blood perfusion did some damage. "Tell them to drop the basket. I'm ready."

I got into the basket with only a little help. I'd rather have ridden up in a loop, like Oscar and the private, but lying quietly in a basket is less humiliating than trying to ride a loop and falling out of it.

The helo landed at a base somewhere. The medics spoke German or something. A translator assured me they would put me under general anesthetic to patch up my arms. I didn't need it and swore at them. I was a trauma expert, and—

They popped a needle in me. I blinked right out.

Chapter Twenty-one

A rough, warm voice prayed at my shoulder. A rough, warm hand held my right hand. I couldn't feel the left hand and opened my eyes in a panic to look for it. It lay atop a sheet with a temporary cast encasing my forearm.

Pins had been taped to my fingertips and elastic bands ran from the pins to hooks set in the cast. Extensor tendon stretchers. Okay.

I took a breath in relief and looked to the other side at Oscar...not Oscar.

Some other dark-haired marine held my hand and prayed in classical Arabic. He was built like a fullback. He lifted a face as familiar as my father's, down to the wire-rimmed glasses. Hooded eyes bored into mine. "Are you awake or still just goggling the room?"

"Omar."

His eyes softened. "Yes. Do you need water?"

I did. He slid an arm under my shoulders and held a cup for me. The water tasted canned. I drank it anyway. Then he brushed a wrinkle from my pillow and laid me back down.

So this is what Omar looked like as a man. His glasses weren't nearly as thick as our father's, but he wasn't yet thirty, either. "You must take care of your eyes. The weakness…"

"I know. I'm seeing yet another specialist next week."

We looked at one another a while, the years between us dissolving. He'd prayed in Arabic. I hoped that meant he'd forgiven me for teaching him how. Even though some of the lessons had come violently. I should have found a softer way, appealed to his intellect perhaps. So many regrets. So many years.

He cleared his throat. "Blue will be here shortly. We can't believe you found the folks. We've been looking for over two years."

"They'd moved. Ben found them too." I thought of saying where, but the walls were flimsy, and I of all people knew that whatever was said in any part of a hospital would soon be heard in every part of the hospital.

His hand tightened on mine, and his eyes searched mine. He glanced about and whispered one word. "Badal."

"Khallas." It was over.

Again, his eyes searched mine. He nodded shortly.

"Echo, how is he?"

"Hairline fractures at C1/C2 and at C5. I'm told he was in surgery before the swelling set in, though. They're confident he'll see full recovery."

A C5 break was the hangman's fracture. "Is he here?"

"No, Germany. Landstuhl. They have facilities you wouldn't believe."

Germany. I'd been to Berlin once, a gray city with gray-black streets, steel gray water, mottled gray snow, grayish lumpen food, and gray-white skies. "Will I be staying here, or going back to my ship?"

"Here, unless you really want to head back to the ship. I've got the use of a place in Plywood Alley for two weeks. Tomorrow, when you're released, you can come stay there. You've got another ten days on TAD, but my unit's on maneuvers—"

"Cap'n?" A voice rose sharply from beyond the door. "Cap'n Momand?"

Omar rolled his eyes. "You think you can yell any louder, Kilo? This is a hospital."

An officer? My brother was an officer?

Sorrow had been an officer too. Somehow, that part of it struck only now.

A skinny kid poked his head in the door. "Sir, the MPs have Lima and Delta. Remember yesterday some jerks was up in that prayer tower, dropping candy for kids and shooting them with rubber bullets when...uh..."

His pale eyes were fixed on my right hand, folded possessively in my brother's. He gulped and red rushed through his face.

Omar clasped his other hand over mine. "Zarak, this is my radioman, Private Kellner. Kilo, meet my older brother, HM1 Momand. You may call him Doc."

"Oh! Honored to meet you, Doc."

I nodded at him, "Hello, Kilo."

"Cap'n?"

"Go," I told them, extracting my hand from Omar's. "Rescue your men. Come back, if you get a chance, and tell me how it went."

An aide checked my vitals, spoke cheerfully to me in some language that might have been German or Swahili for all I knew, and helped me locate the head. I think I had just agreed to be shaved when Blue arrived: First Lieutenant Mohammed Momand. He looked too much like Echo, and he didn't know what to do with his hands, or where to look, or what to say to me. I shooed away the aide, not before he exchanged a few chipper-sounding words with Blue.

Blue turned a motorcycle helmet over in his hands and set it on a too-narrow shelf overhead. It fell. He caught it and set it again more precisely. It fell again. He stood and put it on the seat. "I'm sorry. I thought y'all could just arrest him."

Him. Tango. "The mission was your idea?"

He shook his head vigorously. "I don't have the pull to authorize any of this. I just knew I couldn't speak enough of the language any more, and I feel like people spit in my food every time I sit down in a restaurant here. Omar's got the local lingo, but he's also got so much fucking responsibility."

He paced to the door, listened at it, and paced back. "You've always been the one who could do things. I knew if anyone could figure out this mess without creating an international incident, you could."

"Blue, come here."

He came to sit on the edge of my cot.

I touched one polished-gold eyebrow. His flinch hurt. "Did I create an international incident?"

He stood and paced. "No. At least not yet. And if things stay quiet another twenty-four, we can all relax a little."

"Then why are you so anxious?"

He quirked a grin. "Well, you're never going to play the piano again."

I laughed, shocked. When would I ever play the piano?

Blue grinned more broadly. Then his face went serious again. "Are you going to disappear on us again? Do you hate us that much?"

That cut deep, twisting a blade in my heart. "Do you hate me?"

"No."

That wasn't a completely true answer. "Are you a Muslim?"

He squirmed. "Not a good one. I...I sing."

I remembered the times I'd beaten him for singing with the radio, for sneaking into the piano room when he thought I couldn't hear and picking out tunes of Godless songs. "I am no longer required to act as your father, Blue. Your soul is your own."

He clasped my hand then and spoke in a rush. "I have a girlfriend. I'd love for you to meet her."

I smiled sadly. A girlfriend, not a wife. But I'd said the truth. His soul was his own, and I no longer had the burden or privilege of forging the weapon he was becoming.

The next day, Omar not having returned yet, I was discharged into Blue's care. I reluctantly let him tie my shemagh for me, and even more reluctantly climbed onto the back of his motorcycle. These things had always terrified me, ever since my first ride had ended in a road rash all along my right side. Luckily, his was a very quiet Japanese machine, not one of those helicopter-loud Harleys. Unfortunately, he decided I needed a tour of the city and took me around for many blocks, bellowing information about this landmark, or the musical taste of the assholes in that Toyota.

Suddenly, I knew where we were. "Stop!"

I climbed off the motorcycle, and Blue killed the engine. A group of laborers was cleaning out the ruins of the shop where I'd sat waiting for my garden seeds. The man who sang wasn't in sight.

The baked mud shell of the place remained, but it stank of wet char. "What happened to the man who was here?"

The foreman, identified by the fact he wasn't holding a shovel, squinted at me, at Blue, and back at me.

I awkwardly pried off my helmet and unwrapped my shemagh for the sake of good manners. "The man, the mujahid with no hands."

"That one? He was neither Sunni nor Shia, and then he became too friendly with the English. And so he met judgment. The boy is gone. The English took the girl. She might live." He shrugged. "Inshallah."

The English meant me and Oscar and the sergeant. Because of us, because of me, that inoffensive man had been killed, probably beaten to death. His little girl was in a hospital or an orphanage, the boy conscripted or sent for brainwashing. The little girl had a grandmother—was she begging beside the road, under one of these innumerable dusty burqas? My stomach twisted, but I kept my tone calm. "Did they bury his hands with him?"

"Of course, of course." He seemed insulted that I'd feel any need to ask.

"Come on," Blue urged. "We need to keep moving here."

I straddled his machine again. They'd given me two weeks here. How many lives could I destroy in that time?

The shack in Plywood Alley smelled of roach spray. Blue threw open both windows. An air conditioner was set in the middle of the front door. I turned the fan on full power.

"Fucking noisy," Blue complained.

Noisy, yes. Did everything require a vulgar epithet, though?

But a week ago I'd been the one throwing *f*-bombs everywhere.

He checked the fridge, tossed a ginger ale to me, and popped the tab on a can of Coke. "I'd say home sweet home, but I've seen better dog kennels."

I sat down at the metal desk in the center of the room and elevated my arm in its sling. The pain pills had worn off—or been vibrated off. I wiped the top of the can, then braced the can with my elbow while picking at the pull tab.

"I swear, Z. You talked to that man like a native."

"I am a native," I said quietly. The tab came up, foaming soda all over the lid of the can.

He paced, fidgeting, looked at me, and paced more.

I watched him. The room had two reading lamps, two unmade racks with linens folded at the foot, two windows, an empty bookshelf, a two-burner stove, the fridge, and the air conditioner in the door. There wasn't a lot to explore. "What aren't you telling me, brother?"

"You found the folks? You really went right over there and found them?"

"The border isn't exactly tight."

"Are they like you used to be? All inshallah, bismillah, alhamdulillah?"

My head hurt. My hand hurt. I sipped at the stinging-cold ginger ale. "Where do you think I got it from? Is this a problem for you?"

He swung his arms, cracking his knuckles against the fridge, and swore. Then he ran his fingers through his spiky white-blond hair. "I've spent all this time trying to prove I can be Muslim yet not be a religious freak. Now I don't know if I meet the standards at all."

I'd had the opposite discussion with a seaman recruit that Chaps brought to me a month ago, one who had just discovered Islam and thought being obedient had to mean being obnoxiously obtrusive. "Saying these things is a cultural norm, not a religious requirement. There are Christians who don't say 'Praise Jesus' out loud five or six times a day, just as there are Christians who do. If you don't pay attention to the words, they're just noises anyway. Their function is to focus your mind where it needs to be."

He grinned crookedly. "The holy words are just noises. I never thought I'd hear you say something like that."

I smiled back, though my head hurt too much to really care whether it looked right. "I'm not a teenager any more. From this side of thirty, I can see the difference between mellowing out and selling out."

He shook his head. "Amazing."

Why was it so easy to talk tolerance here, when outside this plywood enclave any sign of tolerance was grounds for murder?

I wanted to go home, suddenly. If home was a reality for anyone past childhood.

"Are you going to keep volunteering for TADs?"

"I didn't volunteer for his one."

He whirled to face me. "*What!*"

I raised my hand. "Never mind. Yes, I plan to volunteer for more. Getting off the ship is good for me."

Oscar wasn't on my ship. Spending time here was no guarantee of seeing him, but staying on my nice safe ship would guarantee not seeing him. I puzzled over the question of why I wanted to see him, when he called me by my brother's name, and set aside the question. I did want to see him. I wanted to hear his voice, too. I wanted to touch his glossy black hair, wanted to feel his gentle lips and rough hands on me.

And if it was a sin, I'd willingly pay the price.

Blue paced until I asked him to help me make the bed; then he insisted on making it for me. Then he shut and locked the windows, for security. He said he'd be back at 0730 and would bring me coffee and something halal for breakfast.

I smiled. I hadn't had coffee in years. But it was nice of him to think of it.

I took a doubled dose of the medication and lay down. Going to sleep nevertheless seemed to take a long time.

I woke up in the dark with someone in the room. I waited for him to say something, or to attack, or something.

"I nearly got you killed."

Oscar. I relaxed. Really, there was not a single person in the world I would rather wake up to. "By missing the knife? If he had it on him, I missed it too."

"I still don't know where he hid it."

I yawned. "He was over near the packs, the tack. It could have been in there. I didn't search his packs."

"But I know better."

"I know a lot of things, Oscar. That doesn't mean I always put them into practice."

"I want you to know one more thing. I never saw you as any kind of substitute for Bravo. For one thing, he was straight." His tone was raw, harsh. Like he'd been screaming a long time.

"You're not coming down with an upper respiratory infection, are you?"

"A cold? Don't think so."

"Good." For a medical person, I really didn't like being around people with minor ailments. Colds. Bruises. Hangovers. You tell them to just endure it, and they react like you've repealed the entire Bill of Rights.

"Should I leave?"

I thought about it. If an international incident hit the media, he and I would both become pariahs, dangerous people to know. Otherwise, I was probably safe to be around. "It depends. All this could still blow up on us."

His voice went hoarser. "Don't fuck with me. Just answer. Am I welcome?"

I threw back the blanket and welcomed him.

ʊ THE END ʊ

Amber Green

Being a bespectacled were-grammarian as well as a professional paper-pusher, I submerge myself in fiction in an attempt to find high adventure (as opposed to anything involving actual expenditure of sweat), lots of nookie, or sometimes just a reality that makes sense. Really.

Loose Id® Titles by Amber Green

Available in digital format at www.loose-id.com and other online retailers

Khyber Run
Steal Away

* * * *

THE HUNTSMEN Series
Backtrack
Lights Out!
Bareback

Khyber Run *is available in print at your favorite bookseller*

CPSIA information can be obtained at www.ICGtesting.com
Printed in the USA
LVOW060245090412

276733LV00001B/59/P

9 781611 183924